MW00768964

To
Sara & Pierre

Please enjoy. Wa
quick read. An
the tatooed motorc
mama.
I am so glad to me
Juanita
September 2005

Blackhawk

Blackhawk

Gary Hanzak
and
Juanita Mucha

3138 Twin Lakes Dr.
Marietta, GA 30062
770-509-1814

Blackhawk

All rights reserved.
© Copyright 1998 Gary A. John Hanzak

Reproduction in any manner, in whole or in part, in English or in any other languages, in print, electronic, or any other medium, or otherwise without written permission of the publisher is prohibited.

This is a work of fiction.
All characters and events portrayed in this book are fictional, and any resemblance to real people or incidents is purely coincidental.

For information address: GMS Publishing   PO Box 6264
Richmond VA 23230 - 0264

Printing History
First Printing 1998
Second Printing 1998
Third Printing 2000

Printed in the United States of America

ISBN 0-9667535-0-X

For

Mom and Dad

Although he would deny any connection
with the Divine, I need to acknowledge
my writing angel, David Page.

JM

Prologue

LONDON, ENGLAND:

A paraglider made news in February 1994 when he landed on the roof of Buckingham Palace. The man landed on the Palace roof at 7:27 a.m. and stripped.

The *London Times* reported that the London Fire Brigade had been called to check for contamination by radioactivity below the belt. At Charing Cross Police Station, the glider pilot told police that the green paint daubed liberally around his groin was radioactive.

After examinations and tests, the fire brigade gave the paraglider the all clear.

1

"From the posh world of vintage aeroplane ownership enters Michael Chessie," began the president of Leesburg's Daughters of the American Revolution. "Born of aristocratic parents in Dublin, Ireland, he states his life has been one pleasure
after another.

"He is single. He is rich, and yes, he is good looking. Beware all you bachelorettes. He just might beguile the socks, or more, off you." The group tittered with polite laughter.

"Mr. Chessie is our guest speaker this afternoon, and he will let us in on all the night owl air plane noise. Ladies, let's welcome Mr. Michael Chessie to our community."

Michael rose from his seat next to the podium. He nodded politely to Madam President, then produced his best smile for the ladies. "Wonderful luncheon you've provided, ladies, I'm honored, and a good afternoon to you."

"Aah yes," he thought as he surveyed all the done-up faces, fancy dresses, and gold jewelry before him. "I do hear a couple sighs."

Most emphatically, he did not want to be here. He loathed this display before him. For the best result, however, he tried to fake sincerity as best he could. Maybe his Irish brogue could convince the women that he thought he was in Heaven in the midst of all of them. He finally spoke, "Am I in Heaven? I am but one man in the midst of all this beauty. Life truly is one pleasure after another, isn't it?" The women laughed, enjoying the flattery. A few even applauded.

"The brogue is doing it," he thought. "An American chap wouldn't get away with such nonsense."

"Well, now, you're probably asking yourselves what could an owner of vintage aeroplanes possibly have interesting to say? I'll tell you truthfully, if you've not an interest in wonderful state of the art flying--as it was then--there isn't anything I could reveal that would be of interest to you, at least in that regard.

"I find that one must be passionate about something in life in order to make it veritably worthwhile. Don't you agree?" Michael Chessie took the microphone from its holder. He walked from the back of the lectern to the front of the dais. As he walked, a limp, which he had as a young child, was barely discernible.

"Excuse my back, Madam President and you other lovely ladies sitting with her, but I like to get close to my audience." He paused a moment for effect. "Yes, passion," he continued meeting a woman's eyes who was sitting directly in front of him. Every woman at that table fell in love with his blue eyes. He looked at every one of them.

"I found that when I wanted to save and restore these machines, I was in the recycling business. Very popular today, but not so when I first began my restorations. My passion, I've found, is not just to recycle and restore beauty, but to make a profound and lasting impact on the world, suggesting, even showing, how it ought to be."

Chessie walked over to the next table and sat down in one of the empty chairs. He was speaking to the group, but each person felt he was speaking to her.

He looked to the woman at his right. "Perhaps you've figured out that maybe I'm not just passionate about aeroplanes, yes?"

The woman sized him up and said, "I certainly hope so. I don't much get into planes except to fly somewhere." Michael Chessie laughed with the rest of the women, and slapped his leg for emphasis. "Madam, what a lovely voice you have. The lilt is musical."

"I like yours, too. Only mine's called a drawl."

"Well, thank you," he said smiling, then turned to the woman on his left. "I also have a passion about the environment, and that's why I've bought a farm here in Leesburg."

"Get me through this circus," he thought. "If I can convince these women that I'm conscientious in what I'm doing, they'll convince their husbands, and the rest of the community will follow."

He spoke again, "I own some apple orchards here, and I'm studying the effects of acid rain on the harvest."

He got up and began to walk back to the podium, taking in another table. He spoke of how he seeded clouds at various times of the day and night to collect data. The night flights were more noticeable because there was less extraneous noise contributed by impatient traffic or screaming children. He spoke of the balsa trees on the top of the mountain that fell over from the acid rain. Perhaps his study would help find a solution to save other trees, fruits and food crops.

The talk was only fifteen minutes, but the impact he made would remain longer. He liked the way he walked and talked. That held the listener's attention, and made his topic stick more poignantly. Most of the audience believed he was sincere.

Chessie sat down and the president asked if there were any questions. There was one. "Mr. Chessie, we couldn't help notice that you walked with a slight limp. Is there a story there? But if we're intruding, you don't have to answer."

"No, no, no, I'd love to answer," he lied, smiling handsomely. He cleared his throat. "About twenty years ago, I was testing an aircraft I had acquired, and it took a rather rough landing. One might say it crashed, and I limp as a result of the injuries sustained."

"Why wouldn't _you_ say it crashed?" asked another woman.

"Nothing on the plane, except my leg, broke," he stated simply. "It never mended properly."

2

Leaving the Hunt Club, after his talk to the lovely Daughters of the American Revolution, Michael Chessie whispered, "Thank goodness that's over!" The story of the plane crash and his resulting limp was the frosting he needed. Nothing like inspiring sympathy to get what you want.

His car was waiting. He jumped in, then conservatively exited the club. Out of sight of the white-gated entrance, Chessie screeched his tires and ran the back roads to his farm.

He phoned Frank at the laboratory from his car phone. "Frank, Chessie here. Just finished my fricking social commitment with the ladies."

"Were you charming?"

"Hell, yes. The whole lot would have jumped into bed with me at a snap of my finger. And I might add, that I would have performed magnificently as long as I avoided getting knocked unconscious with all the gold bangles."

"That bad?"

"That bad. How many more people must I convince of our sincere efforts to save the earth?"

"Today's luncheon was your last engagement. Hopefully you'll receive favorable press and that's always good for the cause."

"Right. See you in fifteen minutes."

Michael Chessie had one overriding ambition in life: to build his Ulster Protestant heritage into an unassailable rock with the Britain he had done so much to defend. He had the means, the motivation and the money.

Mr. Chessie was a charismatic individual with infinite networks. Born into a crystal empire, he had an eye for beauty and perfection. Ireland was his home with his ancestry heralding from Ulster, in Northern Ireland. His great ancestors originally began the glass cutting and etching operation in Belfast. The more industrialized north had greater taxes to pay, whereas in the agricultural south they were less. They moved to the southern counties for reduced cost and ease of labor recruitment. The move proved to be lucrative from the outset and very practical in view of the political situation referred to as "The Troubles."

Going back to the year 1154 and to King Henry II, who was given Ireland by Pope Hadrian IV, he and his succeeding monarchs imposed rule on that country. Being a Catholic country, it came as no surprise when civil war broke out as Protestantism was forced upon them. Through the centuries there has been much religious intolerance and a great deal of difficulty as a result. In the seventeenth century, a group of Scots was sent to Ireland to help keep the peace. They settled in what is now Northern Ireland. Because they had English royalty backing them, they owed the king their loyalty and considered themselves very much subjects of the crown. They wanted to be under British rule.

Northern Ireland belonged to England and that was that. The Protestants who lived there wanted it to remain Protestant. It was just a handful of misguided terrorists, with nothing better to do than flex their muscles on the Anglican Area, that was making such an impact on the world.

The impact was felt as an outrage in America. Most there knew little of the history of that piece of Ireland, and so felt it was terrible that England should inflict itself on such a tiny bit of an island that wanted to be independent.

And so it is that much money for terrorism is raised in America, sometimes to the tune of two million dollars per year. Under the guise of helping the homeless who are victims of English tyranny, Americans donate money. They are mindless of the fact that most of this money goes to Libya to supply arms to the terrorists who get money for trying to unify Ireland and rid the country of the British.

In the British Parliament in 1912, there was a plan for home rule, where all the counties of Ireland were to be united. The Curragh Mutiny of 1914 almost thrust the entire country into a civil war. It swung the vote in Parliament against reunification, and the plan was never implemented.

Michael Chessie often returned to Northern Ireland to visit friends and relations. Business in the Republic of Ireland was more easily conducted from Dublin, but he still had his heart in Ulster.

Michael had married the beautiful Moira O'Neil. Together they had a child, Timothy. Michael could never forgive himself for not driving his family North that Sunday to visit friends and relatives. He was away on business in Belgium when Michael's father drove Michael's mother, Moira and Timothy to Ulster for the weekend. On the way home, on a Sunday afternoon, while in the Republic of Ireland, the Irish Republican Army mistook the car for a getaway car belonging to a Protestant gang that had blownup a Catholic news agent in that part of the county. They shot the driver, Chessie's father, and the car went off the road, careening over the side of a hill. There were no survivors.

Chessie, ever since that event, never forgave the Irish Republican Army, which was just doing its job. Much of his personal money went toward the Ulster Liberation Front (ULF) to rid the area of anyone wanting it to become part of a unified Ireland. This was done secretively as he did not want his business connected with politics. Nor did he wish to hurt his own social or business relations by having it known that he supported Northern Ireland, while living in the Republic.

It was at an informal dinner party in London that Chessie broke out into a cold sweat upon hearing conversation between Prime Minister of England, Westhall, and President of the United States, Glenelly, about unifying Ireland. Any clandestine information was thought harmless when falling on Chessie's ears. Everyone thought he was ignorant where politics was concerned although they could never figure how such a business genius failed to grasp the fundamentals of government. Chessie always laughed and said that was why he had a legal department. They were paid to tend to those details. Chessie overhearing this covert conversation, realized it was not just between two men, but actually between two countries. To say that these economic and political changes would be radical, would be understating the situation. The extreme and the fanatical would be provoked and he didn't just mean ideas. A civil war of major proportions would take place, which would be just as passionate as the religious wars that took place in any of the Russian or Slavic states during the early '90s.

Michael Chessie and Nigel Westhall were friends from the time they attended Cambridge. Chessie, claiming he didn't have the stomach or the brain for politics kept with family tradition and attended the school of business and economics. Westhall followed a political career. The two were bound by three common interests, good food, fine wine and a good game of golf. It was no accident that much business and politics were mixed on the greens, although Chessie made it a practice to stay clear of the politics. He allowed others in his organization to make recommendations to him, but he always tried to maintain a disinterested outlook.

Once out of university, Chessie went into the family business of manufacturing crystal. He was a real genius in business. He instrumented the merger of his crystal empire with that of the a major porcelain manufacturer. The merger was beneficial to both companies. Where most businesses were folding left and right due to the recession, the crystal and china empire seemed to be growing stronger.

In 1992 when the European Economic Community solidified itself, becoming the European Union, the armchair pessimists in England said that it would never work. It became an economic power to be reckoned with, but not all the countries were benefiting. The United Kingdom was one that suffered.

Of all the countries in the EU, England was the one which moaned and recriminated the most, even prior to 1992. Being an island, almost all raw materials had to be imported, which increased the cost of goods tremendously. Having to stay in line with the other countries' prices, the UK was finding it difficult to keep its head above water in terms of these extra costs.

In the depth of recession, the European Union hoped by uniting economically, each of the member countries would begin to pull itself up by the bootstraps. Most did in fact, but England in particular fell from the recession into a depression.

This was how the prime minister of England and the president of the United States began to plan an economic coup. Nigel Westhall, the prime minister, and Thomas

Glenelly, the president, developed their scheme over a good game of golf and a couple drams of scotch.

Westhall saw no reason for staying with the EU. He wanted out, as well as a majority of English people. After all these years, the United Kingdom received no benefit by having membership with such an elite community. The European Union seemed to have sapped the country of all its economic clout, its power and its strength.

The scheme Whitehall had developed with Glenelly was to join economic forces with North America. North America being Canada, the United States, Mexico and the Central American countries. The agreement was that England, keeping its sovereignty, would not have to pay any tariffs to North America, and North American trade in England would have a reciprocal tariff free stipulation.

There was one stipulation that Glenelly made. It was that along with this newly created economic front, there would be a complete and unconditional reunification of Ireland. Northern Ireland was to be returned to the Republic. Over a casual dinner party, the pact was made. It was up to the prime minister to smooth the way for reunification and put an end to "The Troubles." It was up to the president to incorporate the United Kingdom into NAFTA (North American Free Trade Agreement) creating a new financial alliance.

Glenelly was a second generation American. His ancestors came from Dublin, and it had always been a dream of the family that the island be one, rather than two, countries.

The American vice president and the British Cabinet were not to be told about what was happening with Ireland, although the plan for joining economic forces was to be fully disclosed.

Michael Chessie saw the genius in the financial plan, but the Irish unification went against his grain. Something had to be done, and quickly.

The vice president of the United States had no allegiance or interest in a unified Ireland. If no one knew about the Irish stipulation, the economic plan could be implemented without expediting the controversial political one. The president would be returning to DC in a week. Soon after that, he would be presenting a draft for a new trade agreement to his advisors. "It was a shame," thought Chessie, "that this would have to be delayed."

3

Jay Dawson scrambled to the top of the antenna. "How long did that take?" he called down to his ground crew of one.

"Dawson, you asshole, one of these days you're going to get yourself killed," came the voice over the headset.

"Just give me the statistics, Bubba---how fast?"

"Twenty-seven seconds."

"Yes! That betters my previous record by two seconds," Jay boasted as he began to repair the transmitter.

"Why do you do that?" came the ground voice again.

"Hey--climbing these mothers is boring. Gotta do something to put excitement in the day."

"Yeah, but Dawson, normal assholes don't go straight up hand over hand. They use their feet for leverage."

"Bubba, you worried about me?"

"No. It's just that no one ever taught me how to clean a splattered body from concrete." Jay laughed and continued with the maintenance.

When Jay Dawson had entered the world of broadcasting, he had no idea that it would entail climbing antennae on the top of high mountains. His college roommate had gotten him interested in broadcasting when he had assisted him in producing a program at their college television facility. The program exposed the local small town sheriff's department. The sheriff was pocketing the monies from fines inflicted on the college students. The students investigated it due to the vast inconsistencies: the dollar amounts which were high, the number of students fined, many, versus the number of townies being fined, none, and the reasons for the fines which were ridiculous. What started out as a sociology project ended in a courtroom trial.

The final result was the ousting of the sheriff. They also discovered he was skimming the local fines to redecorate his game room at home. His finished basement had been the monthly scene of a very large and lucrative poker game.

When the old sheriff lost his job, the poker game disappeared. It was still in town, but no one was telling where it had moved. Jay graduated from college and moved out of state, so the mystery was left to the undergraduates.

From that one experience, Jay had gotten a taste for investigative journalism. He became an avid student of broadcasting and journalism. His instinct on wanting to know the other side of the story was the motivating force in getting to the bottom of an assignment. In working through the media system, Jay felt situations were often equalized. When the baddies were exposed, their victims felt somewhat vindicated at seeing the defeat of the malefactors. Often monetary retribution was in order, and that was the topping on the cake as far as he was concerned. More than anything, he wanted to break into a position as an investigative journalist at a network TV station. But he knew that he had some dues to pay.

To complete his degree in broadcasting and get on to that desired position, he became licensed as a first class engineer. On the way, he learned all the technical and electronic workings of every communication device: radio, television, telephone, radar, microwave, electronic transmitting devices like pagers.

That's how he came to be overlooking the top of the world, 100 feet over the top to be exact. Repair work to Jay was mundane, but he was the person at the station who got things working. He was the fastest and most efficient on the staff. He could read a schematic in seconds, and knew why something worked, or didn't work. It was as though his brain understood the electronic physiology of any device.

From on top of this mountain, Jay could see hot air balloons rising in the distance. "I wonder if I could make a pocket radar that could detect objects that far away?" He said it more to himself than to the man on the ground, but the ground responded.

"Geez, Dawson, your brain fixes on the strangest stuff."

"Oxygen's pretty thin up here, Bubba. Does funny things to the old frontal lobes."

"Would you finish and get down here? I'm hungry."

"Coming," responded Jay, and five seconds later, after sliding down the ladder's hand rails, he jumped to the ground, startling his helper. Making his gymnast's two point landing, arms and legs outstretched, brown curly hair blowing wildly around his head, he cheered in Spanish, "Completa!"

"Aren't you ever serious?" asked Bubba.

"Nope, not any more," commented Jay as he put his tools into the van. "There is so much bad happening in this world, that if I let myself think about the seriousness of it all, I'd become a manic depressive. Nope, my job is to enjoy what I do, help some people along the way, and have some fun while I'm at it."

"Your two dimples and charm may have other people fooled at the station, but not me. You're certifiable. You're crazy."

"No I'm not. Crazy was when I was getting a divorce. I'll never do that again. It'll be a long time before I ever contemplate marriage."

"Marriage ain't so bad."

"Well, maybe it is, and maybe it isn't, but I know that I went at it all wrong. I was too selfish to be married. Didn't want anyone cramping my style, and I didn't want to be much a part of her style, either. It was all take and no give, on both our parts. That's no way for any relationship to be. When I find someone who wants to grow old with me, as well as share in our growth spiritually, psychologically, and all that shit, then maybe I'll think about marriage again. Right now, I am not interested in a serious, or a meaningful, relationship. All I want-----"

"Geez, Dawson, enough already. I like it better when you're hanging in the breeze from top of an antenna, not shooting the breeze on top of a soapbox."

4

Bob Gregg sat in his office speculating on what was going to keep him from getting bored in the next few months before retirement. He kept delegating everything so that he could ease out of the position and the building without being called back to explain what was going on. There really wasn't all that much happening that his support team couldn't handle. He was already in the back seat.

Use to taking a more active role, Bob Gregg didn't like just sitting around. His quick thinking made him eager for something daring. Each piece of paper that crossed his desk he saw as an adventure.

Gregg was a master in emergencies. He liked to implement new ideas and use inventions and state of the art prototypes to solve situations. That was how he rose from a lowly national park ranger to district supervisor in the Antiterrorist Intelligence Agency (ATI).

It drove his supervisors nuts. They came to expect the unexpected from him. Nine times out of ten his unconventional methods worked. They tolerated his success, but they didn't endorse his methods.

One's first impression of Bob Gregg could be deceptive. Nothing of his looks told you he was unconventional except his ties. Always silk, and always a work of art, the tie in his outfit caught your eyes and your speech first. Double breasted suits, wingtips, and a close cropped haircut caught you thinking of *Gentlemen's Quarterly*. Whispers behind his back questioned what he wore for underwear. Disappointment and surprise would likely surface if they discovered they were plain white boxers.

Another dimension of Bob Gregg was his compassion. He quietly cared that some of his less fortunate associates had made it to the legions of the homeless, now in epidemic numbers in DC and in America in general. Their plight moved him so, that he started an underground network of people who could help these folks.

The silent coordinating force behind the movement, Bob Gregg wanted no recognition, no acknowledgement of his contacts. He felt more could be accomplished if he didn't care who got the credit, so he often stepped aside and let someone with better capabilities do the job.

When he left the building, he was often met by scruffy characters, but scruffy characters approached everyone in DC. It was a fact of life.

Some people doled out $10 worth of quarters, a quarter at a time, to beggars until the supply was gone. Bob Gregg doled quarters and information and in return received more information and satisfaction.

He had the social, medical and teaching professions involved. Industrial giants played their part, as well as the churches. It was easy to get the ball rolling. Many of these entities were eager to circumvent the status quo. They operated efficiently, and with a minimum of red tape, for the numbers of people without homes, jobs and/or families. It was all underground, and although no one made a penny, everyone profited.

Bob Gregg started it and quietly bowed out as more proficient organizers stepped in. He maintained his connections, though, as he never knew when he was going to need them. Occasionally, he would receive a call for advice----how he would recommend a situation be handled or directed.

Unless you were involved in this network, you didn't know that Bob Gregg was. Most couldn't even guess at his compassionate side. The stern look on his face was generally all business and belied any of his kind traits.

Friends, though, knew that there was charm, wit and a great salesman behind the facade. With the way he resolved things he needed a good command of the oratory arts to explain his techniques.

Leaning back in his chair, he tried to imagine what he would do as a retired Antiterrorist Intelligence agent. ATI didn't have him active in the field anymore. He was more of a consultant. "Maybe I could reactivate and spy on suspected spies," he chuckled to himself at the intrigue of it all. "Man, we really do tangle ourselves in webs, don't we. I'll have to lose some of this weight, though," he said getting up from his desk to quit for the day.

"Going home, Martha," said Bob Gregg to his secretary as he passed her desk.

"Good night, Mr. Gregg. Public TV is showing your documentary again tonight."

"Oh?" he sounded and looked pleased, then his face did battle with itself, and pleased changed to dejected. "Well, the scoundrels who deface public property won't be watching it, so what's the use of reeducating the already educated?"

"Reinforcement, Sir?"

"Reinforcement?"

"Mr. Gregg, you have exposed the American public to some of their architectural heritage. The beauty of that program illustrates the art and science of those buildings. I believe they would be outraged if they knew that vandalism and public defacement were increasing. A campaign is in order here," Martha pounded her desk for emphasis.

"Campaign? Reinforcement? Martha, you sound as though you're staging a war."

"If it takes a war----"

"Speaking of wars, this tired old war horse, is going home and having a scotch. I'll see you in the morning."

As he left for his home in Bethesda, Bob Gregg reflected on his documentary. Thanks to the help of Jay Dawson, who helped him produce this piece of work, the documentary was excellent. It was now being used in schools to educate the young in the appreciation of America's architecture. It was a great teaching tool, but there was no evidence of increased public awareness, or outrage to the defacing of public property.

Gregg was frustrated with the public. If it were left to him, entrance to all national parks or monuments would be by membership only, like his country club.

Bob Gregg's thoughts about his job, and his pet peeve left his head and were replaced by thoughts of food. His wife, Agnes, was at home, and had prepared him a wonderful meal. Then his thoughts soured. Maybe it wasn't so wonderful. His wife was trying to get him to lose weight for health reasons, so maybe it was going to be a yuk vegetable dish. Then again, it could be Italian. His mind dwelled on that so he wouldn't feel depressed about vegetables. He couldn't complain, though. Anything Agnes cooked, even vegetables, was always tasty, just not always filling.

"Retirement may be opening a restaurant in DC with my wife as partner and chef," he thought. "No, that would tie us down too much. If we become restaurateurs, we'll have to hire a manager and a chef. That way Agnes and I could travel and spend the restaurant's profits. I'll have to wait to see what Agnes says. With my luck, she'll want a vegetarian restaurant, and that'll take all the fun out of it."

5

No one seemed interested in the TV network's expose that the British army and security services were up to their noses in the worst terrorist atrocities since the second world war.

There was the quadruple bombing of main streets in rush-hour Dublin and Monaghan in May 1974 killing thirty-three. It was the work of a paramilitary Protestant gang, equipped and trained by British army and intelligence officers. The gang was the Mid-Ulster Brigade of the Ulster Liberation Force (ULF), and its leader, the man described as Blackhawk, has continued murdering ever since.

A civil rights leader in Portadown, was shot dead at his door in October 1973 when two men asked his wife if they could have a word with him. The dead man's wife later identified Blackhawk's group, but the Blackhawk was never found.

A pop group, of no particular political persuasion was stopped in July 1975 at a road block near the border by a group of men wearing British Army uniforms. A bomb was put in the van and it went off almost instantaneously killing the man who put it there, and his assistant. Both members were from the Mid-Ulster Brigade of the ULF. The rest of the gang opened fire on the fleeing defenseless pop group. Three of the six were killed. All members of the gang were sentenced to life in prison and are still there. The Blackhawk, who supervised and master minded the operation, was never apprehended.

One of the very few Catholic policemen in Northern Ireland was shot dead at his door in Cushendall in February 1977. He was investigating links between the ULF and the Royal Ulster Constabulary special branch. He believed they were working together to rob banks. A special branch officer at Blaymena was arrested and charged with the murder and a number of armed robberies. He was acquitted of the murder. In a special interview with this man, he stated the Blackhawk was behind the murder. The Hawk's presence was often felt, but seldom seen. The Blackhawk was never found, arrested or charged.

In April of 1977 a Catholic shopkeeper at Ahoghill near Balymena, in Northern Ireland was gunned to death when asked to get some medicine for a sick child. Of the four assassins, two were duly convicted of murder. Both got life and are now out of prison. In evidence, one of them admitted to being part of the Blackhawk's group.

The police force of Northern Ireland had been asked why the Blackhawk was no where to be found. One of the officers pleaded it was to safeguard the security of the operational strategy in that county.

A reporter for the *Sunday World* who was investigating Protestant assassinations, was seriously wounded by a gunman who came to his home in May 1984. It was not disclosed that the gunman had been sent by the Blackhawk.

Blackhawk's gang, whose other two leaders are two Portadown gunmen known as Eric the Red and Shorty, carried out the Dublin bombings and had gone on killing Catholics at random and without impunity. The gang was responsible for the murders of three youths in a mobile sweet shop at Braigavon in March 1991.

Blackhawk's gang gets most of its weapons from South Africa. In April 1992, two South African military intelligence officers were expelled from Britain after they met the gang and discussed the supply of arms.

The South African connection had been encouraged by British intelligence. In 1987, a British informer in the Command Council for Protestant Ulster (CCPU) sent a British Army intelligence agent to South Africa to seek arms for the paramilitaries.

When the arms arrived later that year, it came in two batches, one for the British Army, and the other for the ULF. The army consignment was seized, but the ULF assignment got clean away to the Blackhawk's gang.

No one has actually seen Blackhawk, but his presence is keenly felt. Most of his directives are carried out by a second or even a third party. There is usually no contaminating of the directive, because the delivering parties know that they won't be given a second chance to screw up.

Rumor has it that the Blackhawk's family was mistaken for a ULF terrorist group, and annihilated by the IRA. The family was his wife, mother, father, and young son out for a Sunday drive in the country. Unfortunately, their car matched that of the ULF's get away vehicle, and it was blown to bits. It seems the Blackhawk's reputation was born about this same time.

The actions of the Blackhawk are very much protected like the actions of the Godfather in the Mafioso. The Blackhawk avenges any misconduct on Protestant Ireland. The Protestants voluntarily swear allegiance to him.

His presence is there to protect as well as intimidate the Irish Republican Army. The Mid-Ulster Brigade of the Ulster Liberation Force (ULF) exists to remove the Catholic menace from their counties in a more active way than the British Army, and the Blackhawk lends his assistance.

6

She was lust in a little black dress. The neckline was high, the hemline as short as a pair of black tights could decently allow, and the sleeves were rivaled in length only by her legs.

And the legs, yes, it was her legs that caught Agent Stover's eye. Fancying himself a confirmed leg and ass man, a self espoused expert, Stover rated this pair well above average. "Actually," he thought to himself, "the hell with putting them above average, I'd rather put them above my head."

Taking a drink from his draft, Stover surveyed the rest of the bar from over the rim of his beer mug. "Not a bad place for a crusty, old neighborhood bar. A few regulars, friendly service, and oh, what a pair of legs." The bar maid was taking an order at a table, bending at the waist just enough to let the hemline expose a little more upper thigh.

Tearing his eyes away from the view he remonstrated himself for being such a pervert, but he had a grin on his face.

The grin broadened to a smile as he noticed the two zit-faced kids sitting at the bar with their eyes glued on her behind. No doubt they had done the bar maid every which way from Sunday in their daydreams. Periodic jabs and rolled eyes passed between the friends as they enjoyed their drink. He questioned whether they were old enough to be drinking in the first place, but that was not his jurisdiction.

Resuming his appreciation of the bar maid, Stover caught her eyes and held her gaze for several seconds. "The sorry thing is," Stover thought, "she knows exactly what effect she is having. Without saying a single word, she has added twenty to fifty dollars to her tip. Hell, if we were in DC she would have added ten times that to her tip and probably received a few secretarial job offers to boot."

Amanda, the bar maid, watched as the two hayseed kids from the bar, ploughed through the exit. She smiled knowing that her body and especially her legs had the desired effect not only on the ploughboys but on the clean-cut man sitting at the end of the bar, her target.

He saw her smile and took it as an invitation. When she was close enough, Stover asked, "Can I buy you a beer?"

"The bar is closing. Besides, I don't drink with total strangers, Mister," she said still smiling.

"The name is Stover, John Stover. Now I'm not a total stranger."

"You're not a total stranger, Mr. Stover, but you are totally strange. What's with the short haircut? You airing out your scalp or something?"

He laughed, "I'm afraid it goes with the job."

"Oh? and what might that be?"

"Uh, let's just say it's community relations."

"Mmm, some relations can be good," she said sliding herself onto the barstool next to the community relations man, "but I have to get home. Busy day tomorrow."

"What? Why?" He was a little surprised.

He looked offguard she thought. "He probably thinks I'm easy." As she got down from the barstool, she placed her hand on his thigh to assist herself to the floor. "I'll bet you have really good relationships. Would you like to have one with me?" She looked at him flirtatiously and walked to the door. She stopped before opening it and looked back at Agent Stover over her shoulder. She waved and said, "See you later, John Stover," and went out the door.

"Ha!" thought Stover. "I'll bet she thinks I'm going to follow her. I can't believe I'm not, but as she said: busy day tomorrow." He nursed what was left of his beer and left as the bartender was turning out the lights. When Stover got outside, he could not believe she wasn't waiting. He had even rehearsed a rejection speech.

Amanda Shahey, on the other hand, could not believe he had not followed her. She wanted him and she knew that he desired her. She walked home, alone, planning her busy day.

* * *

It was early Saturday morning when John Stover drove to find a paper. He regretted not going after the femme fatale of the night before, but her flirtation smacked of danger. That type of peril he didn't need on this assignment, even if he was a lonely government man.

Stover drove an unmarked blue sedan. He had been in the Winston-Salem area for a day following a lead on a killing.

A colleague on the trail of some highly classified information had been shot dead on Interstate 77 outside Rockhill, South Carolina two nights ago. Witnesses said someone on a motorcycle blew him away. Forensics said it was a .44 Magnum.

The agency didn't know what the individual looked like, only that the biker was dressed in black and was seen heading north on a large bike. To date he had seen dozens of cycles, but none that looked out of the ordinary.

As he pulled away from the curb, a large Harley roared past at the intersection 500 feet ahead of him. Already prejudiced, Stover knew this was the type of bike he expected to be tracking.

He raced ahead to the stop sign, ignored it, and took the same direction as the Harley. Harleys in themselves aren't suspicious, so he would just follow this character, pull his badge and ask him a few questions.

It wasn't going to be easy. Motorcycles are built for maneuverability, and could out race most four wheel vehicles on any given day.

It was early morning and the highway was clear, so he pushed the Ford to ninety. Two miles outside of town, the gap was closing. Was it his imagination or was his prey slowing?

Around the curve in the road, he lost sight of his chase. As he got round the bend, the motorcycle had disappeared. Coming up fast was a side access. The highway sign indicated it was a quarry road. Could the bike have made a diversion?

The dust screen rising above the quarry road was a dead give away for the direction the cycle took.

Braking quickly and turning sharply, the car stayed on the road but only with two wheels. Through the skid, the agent kept the vehicle under control and avoided the ditches on both sides of the dirt track.

He accelerated to ninety and prayed nothing was coming from the other direction. Visibility was zero. As far as he knew there wasn't even a road beneath him.

All of a sudden he burst through the dirt storm and into the clear open air. Dead ahead of him was the open quarry.

His stomach was in his boots, but he slammed on the brakes anyway. Stover turned the wheel to avoid going over the edge. "Jesus," he realized, "this had to be the killer. If I live to complete the paperwork, I'll add cunning and coldhearted to this guy's description."

The car slid sideways toward the fast approaching abyss. Stover jumped from the car and rolled as the blue sedan pitched over the side.

He went for his gun and a tremendous pain pierced his side. He couldn't make his arm work. Lifting his head, Stover tried to locate the Harley. It was on its side, where the dust storm had ended.

Coming his way was the figure dressed in black, holding a helmet in one hand and a gun in the other.

"Jesus," he moaned, "it's you!"

"Sorry relations couldn't have been better."

The report of a .44 Magnum is deafening.

7

He was tired of seeking relationships with women-----
tired of the rejection and tired of the energy needed to sustain
such foolishness.

Jay Dawson was a broadcasting engineer for ABS
Broadcasting outside Richmond, Virginia. He had to be
available twenty-four hours a day, weekends and holidays
included, in the event a transmitter or studio equipment
failed.

He was tired of fixing. He wanted action, and he felt
investigative journalism was his niche.

To relieve the stress and to release his creative
tendencies, he fiddled with electronic gadgetry.

Some people needed a schematic to understand the
flow of power for an electric device, toaster, TV or computer.
Not so for Jay. He could envision schematics. As a result he

always discovered miracle cures for down equipment at the station.

Always building something, Jay's last project was an electric camera built into his telescope. His current project was a hand held radar device. There was no immediate or practical application for the instrument. Since there were hand-held computers, he thought it would be cool to have a pocket radar. The next time he was out repairing something on top of an antenna, he was going to have it with him, in case he saw any hot-air balloons.

It was Friday night and Dawson just wanted to be alone. Not wanting to impress anybody, or work at polite or clever conversation, he just wanted to be by himself.

Tonight, in the corner of McDougal's Bar, he was content to watch the people play at being more or less than they really were, depending on whom they wanted to impress. From his philosophical position, what Jay observed was very amusing. Common laborers became millionaires, secretaries became movie stars, lawyers became farmers.

Leaning back in the chair, Jay was ready to remain unsociable, until she approached him. Although just a barmaid, something unique about her declared here was no ordinary barmaid.

Brown hair hung in waves down the middle of her back. Dark lashes framed the largest darkest eyes he had ever seen. She was of medium height and build and the short black skirt revealed a great pair of legs.

The high collar and long sleeves of her costume lent an air of innocence. Dazzled, he wasn't going to try to overawe her. He hoped she wouldn't engage him in conversation.

"Hi, can I get you something?"

"Yeah, I'll take a Budweiser."

"OK."

That was the end of the conversation. When this beautiful creature returned he thanked her, and relaxed into sipping beer and listening to the country western music. He tried to watch the clientele, but couldn't keep from watching her.

She was a good barmaid, catching his eye before he had to catch hers. Being good looking and a good waitress most definitely earned you a good tip. None of his three beers came with conversation.

Without ordering it, a fourth beer appeared, and only then did the talk begin.

"Here's another beer. It looked like you might be wanting one."

"Thanks. You read my mind."

"By the way, you aren't gay are you?"

"What! What do you mean?" Jay's chair came tumbling forward from its perched position.

"Well, in the short time I've worked here every guy who comes into this place tries to hustle me. You don't even look interested. I don't know whether to be insulted or amused."

"Well, don't feel insulted. You're damned attractive. It's just that I'm tired of looking for a meaningful relationship to discover it's casual as hell."

"Yeah, I know what you mean. It's really difficult to find someone you can just feel comfortable with, and still have great sex, right?"

"There you go reading my mind again," he grinned.

"I'll leave you to your misery," she laughed walking away to tend to the other customers. He thought about this short exchange. Could it be that women got tired of this game, too?

After the fourth beer, it appeared that Jay might close the place. He left a great tip and wasn't at all surprised when the barmaid said she hoped to see him again. Then he indulged her request.

"My name is Jay."

"Nice to meet you. I'm Amanda."

"I'm going over to the Rocks tomorrow, Amanda. Would you like to go along?"

"Sure. I'll meet you at that little coffee shop on Main Street about ten o'clock, okay?"

"Great. See you tomorrow."

He thought it was both wonderful and crazy. She was gorgeous, and they were just going to be friends.

On the way home he felt pretty good about himself and very glad he decided to seek solitude that evening. He wondered how he managed to fall into these things.

The next day he went over to the cafe to meet Amanda. Walking into the shop her presence was not apparent. Was she late? No, he was late. How come she wasn't there? The answer came straight at him. Gasping, he couldn't believe it. Amanda, the demure barmaid from the previous evening, had transformed.

Walking toward him was someone with the same long sweeping lashes framing the same great eyes, but there was nothing innocent looking about her. This female was wearing a pair of skintight leather trousers, high boots and a fringed black leather jacket zipped down just far enough to expose some cleavage. Her hair didn't hang. It was every-where in all directions all at once.

"Hey, Jay," came the greeting.

"Amanda!" His eyes bulged in disbelief as he choked on her name.

"A little different image from last night, eh?"

"A little?" but quickly he amended, "but you look terrific. You've taken me by surprise. Leather wasn't at all what I was expecting."

"Jay, I'm not at all what anyone expects," she laughed. "Let's have some coffee before we leave."

Amanda sat down straddling the chair. She wondered if Jay was going to bolt. He had thought about it but decided to sit, hoping the coffee would bring him to his senses. For a second time in twenty-four hours he wondered how he managed to fall into these things.

Sipping coffee, Dawson noticed something green on Amanda's shoulder beneath her leather jacket. "Is that a tattoo?" he asked preparing himself for another surprise.

"Yep, it is." Moving her jacket off her shoulder, the tail of a green dragon appeared. Unzipping her jacket and taking it off her left arm, she allowed more of the tattoo to be seen. The tail was wrapping around her arm, and as she began to turn away from Jay, the body of the dragon was on her back. Jay could see that she was removing her jacket, and she was naked beneath the jacket. A hush fell over the cafe and Jay knew all the rest of the patrons were staring.

Throwing a couple dollars onto the table, he helped Amanda back into her jacket and then swiftly pushed her out the door. He couldn't get into the car fast enough.

"I don't believe you," he said laughing, hoping for some comic relief. "You gave those folks a free show."

"Oh, it'll give them something to talk about, but you have got to see my dragon." She turned her back and removed her jacket. Tattoos weren't particularly attractive to Jay, especially tattoos on women, but this dragon was a real work of art. It covered her entire back, with the tail wrapping around one of her arms and the head resting on the opposite shoulder. It truly was spectacular. Once again, he was dazzled.

On her forearm there was the brand name Harley-Davidson in scroll. Seeing he was interested in the artwork, she decided to let him see her other tattoos. He stopped her when she began to unzip her trousers.

"That's ok, Amanda, I'll see them some other time. Let's get to the Rocks."

The rest of the day was pretty uneventful after that spectacular unveiling of the morning. The Rocks were the Rocks, the scenery still the same. Amanda didn't react to any of it. Jay guessed she had been all over the country and had seen more spectacular sights.

When curiosity about the Harley-Davidson tattoo got the better of Jay, Amanda explained, "I ride a Harley, but it's in the shop for repairs. That's the reason for working at the bar. I travel across country with a group of bikers. As soon as I pay for the repairs, I'll catch up with them."

That she was a biker should have aroused his suspicions. He wasn't going to be too hasty to judge someone just because they ran with a gang of motorcyclists. He was a little partial to motorcycles himself, and often fantasized himself a freewheeler.

At the end of the day Amanda asked if he'd like to go into the mountains the next day.

"Sure," he said.

"Good, I'll pick you up."

"Your Harley fixed?"

"No, a friend left me his wheels."

After giving directions to his house, Jay and Amanda parted company. The next morning she picked him up as arranged arriving in a pickup truck jacked up so high you needed a ladder to get into it.

"Where we headed, Amanda?" Jay asked hoisting himself into the cab.

"Oh, we're going to see some dandy views." In short order they were on the freeway headed toward the Blue Ridge Mountains.

"Reach into the glove compartment and get the map," Amanda instructed. Opening the glove compartment, there in plain view was a .44 Magnum. Jay's first instincts were to jump from the truck, but his brain reminded him that the truck was going eighty miles per hour. Chances were that he'd be killed. He began to laugh hysterically, realizing he might be killed anyway. Again the thought hit him. How did he manage to fall into these things?

It was difficult for Amanda to miss Jay's facial expression and the hysterical noise. "Don't worry," her voice was offhanded, "a girl needs protection on the road. It's not meant for you."

"Yes, a girl needs protection, but isn't a Magnum a bit of overkill?"

Then she got more somber than Jay thought any person should ever get, especially a girl who looked like her, despite her tattoos. "You would never believe it, Jay."

His journalistic instincts wanted to hear the details, but his more vulnerable self was terrified to know. Suddenly, he heard himself say, "Are you in any trouble?"

She shrugged her shoulders. "Some guy was bothering me, so I shot him."

"Oho." He knew he believed it and what's more, he was certain he didn't want to know the details.

"I don't know if I killed him, though. I left. Makes you wonder about the company you keep doesn't it?" her laugh returned. "Don't worry, Jay. It's not loaded. Besides we're just friends, not impressing one another, just relaxing with each other's company, right?"

For some reason he wasn't reassured. His relaxation was camouflaged by his white knuckles.

Once in the mountains, the couple hiked a couple miles to a stream. The forest was peaceful, unlike Jay's stomach. Amanda had brought the gun.

She set up targets on the opposite bank of the stream. When she returned, she loaded the gun. Standing some twenty-five yards away, she shot the targets in turn and didn't miss one.

Standing behind a .44 is almost as deadly as standing in front of one. Its recoil can knock a mid-sized man down, but it didn't even bother her small frame.

Reloading, she handed the gun to Dawson. He needed a couple lessons. Once he could shoot without getting knocked off his feet, he began to enjoy it. The more he shot the more exhilarated he felt. The feeling was power. No wonder some people go mad when they hold a weapon. When he started to feel a bit giddy he remembered they hadn't eaten lunch.

Amanda had planned ahead and packed a picnic complete with wine. Once Jay realized that she wasn't going to kill him, he began to relax.

When the rest of the afternoon was spent talking, Jay found that Amanda had a compassionate soul. He could see it when she presented how she would resolve all the world's problems and in her reason for man's existence.

When Amanda dropped him at home, she said, "I like you, Jay. You have the right blend of smoothness and rustic charm. Don't change. Beneath your innocent facade is a streak of wickedness."

"Look who's talking," he countered.   "See you, Amanda. Thanks for the outing."

As usual, when Friday came, you could find Jay in his favorite bar.   Amanda wasn't there.   The barkeep, MacDougal, said she had enough money for her bike and was moving on. He for one would miss her because there was a definite increase in business while she was waitress. Dawson drank his customary four beers, listened to some country western music, watched the other living souls deal with their assigned roles, then left.

While washing his car the next day, Jay heard the engine of a Harley coming up the road. No doubt it was Amanda. She motored up the drive and stopped the bike, but didn't get off. You'd never believe a female was riding that great monster of a thing. Taking off her helmet, she extended her hand.

"Just came around to say good-bye."

"What a fantastic bike," he said taking her hand.

"Well, I'm off. Maybe I'll see ya 'round."

"Sure, take it slow, Mandy."

She hesitated. "No one has called me that since my Mom..." she trailed off. Only the briefest hint of grief registered behind her eyes. Recovering, she said, "Well, yeah, take it easy, Jay. See ya." Donning her helmet, she revved the engine, then rode off as if to beat a hasty retreat.

So much had been left undisclosed. What a mystery, this woman, Amanda: not all was as it seemed. "There's something regrettable about this relationship," thought Jay. "I never got to see the rest of her tattoos."

8

It is not uncommon for the political and social elite to gather periodically and jockey to improve their positions in the pedigreed circles in which they circulate. Washington, DC is no different except those that are "in" and those that are "out" change at a much quicker pace than the rest of America.

Major social upheaval takes place at least every four years, resulting each time as the mantle of power is handed from one political party to the other and back again. New names are added to lists, old names are taken off, old topics of conversation become taboo and new topics replace them.

In ringing the changes every four years, if one isn't quick enough to catch on, one can be caught very short. The view from the outside makes one's head reel. Fast paced and fickle are the fates.

The one constant in Washington life is the annual invitation to Michael Chessie's farm in rural Virginia. To receive an invitation there is a feather to be worn proudly in one's hat.

Partiers in a party town found Chessie's gatherings absolutely boring. Individuals invited did not discuss politics, money or power. They already possessed one, two, or possibly all three of these. Leesburg, Virginia is a place where these topics took a vacation. There was a greater chance that the topic of conversation would be the proper manner to fillet a trout rather than the manner in which a piece of legislation was making its way through congress.

Partiers expecting the usual "bevy of babes" from the current madam of choice or a supply of the latest designer drug were in for a disappointment. If they were smart they subordinated their vices for a day and participated in good food, good talk and good drink. The more fortunate might rub elbows with presidential cabinet members, a few congressional leaders, perhaps a model or two.

One had better be prepared to discuss matters of casual importance, or flying, a Chessie passion. Those not smart enough to catch on were quickly ostracized, or bored, and soon departed much to everyone's relief. Usually, the name was quickly deleted from any future lists.

Michael Chessie preferred it this way: simple plans, simply worked. Give everybody a chance to decompress and forget the worries of the day or the weight of their office. Let them enjoy themselves. "Once they get back inside the beltway, let them try to outmaneuver each other," Chessie thought. "When they are here, relaxation is the operative word. Should I need a business favor, or information, the probability will be much greater to receive it if I show these people a truly relaxed outing."

The party also served as an observation deck from which Chessie could view all the personalities and how they interacted.   "You never know when you might need to call on someone for a special favor."

Vice President Kershaw had been attending Chessie's function for a few years.   Chessie and Kershaw could be overheard easily conversing about ceramics, a Chessie heritage and a Kershaw hobby.

Whether it was debating the air superiority of the Allied Forces during World War I or the use of high tech fibers in aviation, Chessie and Secretary of State Blankenship could go on for hours about aviation. The passion of these two men for flying was well known. As the World War II generation of leadership made its way through positions of authority in both houses of Congress, the number of veterans at this annual gathering telling old war stories became a common sight.

Now that the Viet Nam generation was also in seats of power, the two generations were often found debating tactical strategies.

"That's all right, boys," Chessie thought as he observed the circles of conversation. "Relive the glory days while you can. If you continue to relive the past, the future will overtake you, and the future may not be yours."

Thomas Glenelly, before occupying the oval office, had been a guest once or twice at Chessie's. As a rising, sharp-minded prosecutor, Chessie foresaw the political possibilities this young man possessed. Chessie added Glenelly's name to his list. Since becoming president, however, Glenelly had declined the invitation with a vague promise of "perhaps next year, if the luck of the Irish holds."

"Michael, you have outdone yourself again," Secretary Blankenship said clapping him on the shoulder and walking into the antebellum mansion.

"Yes, I believe it has been another unabashed success. There will be a number of guests staying the night. Will you be among them?" asked Chessie escorting the secretary into his library.

"No, I don't think so, thanks just the same. You know, Michael, my investments this year have really turned a handsome profit. You've done a marvelous job managing my trust."

"No need to thank me. My broker is the one with all the insights. We have indeed been most fortunate this year. There have been no major losses and all of our speculative ventures have panned out in our favor." Chessie poured two scotches and handed one to the secretary.

Secretary Blankenship began again after sipping his scotch. "There is one more major venture to be made and the time is nearing when that undertaking will have its maximum payoff. I hope your investors will be prepared when the time comes to act."

"Mr. Secretary, my advisers and counselors are hand picked and are in training even as we speak. Given forty-eight hours, the assets needed to accomplish our goals can be deployed, vested, and if necessary liquidated to maximize our return."

"Fine, Michael, just fine. As long as our assets are covered, so to speak."

"They are indeed covered, Sir." The two men clinked their glasses conspiratorially.

9

It was Friday night and Jay Dawson was in the bar musing over the platonic relationship that developed with Amanda. Although she had ridden off into the sunset on her Harley he felt deeply self-satisfied that it had not turned into a sexual encounter. He allowed the smugness to envelope him as he watched the old and new clientele rain in.

Mic the barkeep was shorthanded so Jay decided to help him. Not waiting for his permission, he just started drawing beers. Tending bar was how he had worked his way through college, so the tap side of the bar wasn't new to him.

For a Friday, this was a respectable crowd. Most everyone was relaxed and sympathetic with the lack of waitresses. No one pressured for immediate service.

It was a good thing, too, because it looked like Mic was going to fall apart. After the first wave of customers, he should have relaxed, but he was far more fidgety than Jay had ever seen him.

Mic was a good barkeep. Playing his role well, he listened to your troubles never commiserating or condemning. Although he could keep his end of the conversation going, he never disclosed anything about himself, so no one knew very much about him. In fact no one seemed to know if Mic was his first name or a short version of his surname, McDougal.

Mic had one of those ageless faces. The lines told you he had to be over forty, but his jet black hair unblemished by gray didn't help reveal how much over forty. He could have been sixty.

McDougal was shorthanded before, and he could laugh or talk his way through most tight spots. Dawson was curious why tonight was different. If he stayed long enough Jay hoped to get an answer. His patience and curiosity were both rewarded.

After the rush at the bar, Jay returned to his corner. Instead of watching the patrons, he watched Mic. He seemed to fidget more as he knew Jay was watching. Two men walked up to the bar and waited to speak to him. From their backs they looked like two ordinary businessmen, but their faces reflected in the mirror behind the bar told a different story. Their hard faces held a severe unsmiling expression. There eyes were watchful.

The barkeeper nodded "yes", pointed in Jay's direction, then walked away to wait on some paying customers.

The two men turned and walked toward Dawson. Jay felt the hackles on the back of his neck rise.

"Mr. Jay Dawson?" one of them asked stiffly.

"Yes, that's me," he replied with as much calm as possible.

"We're placing you under arrest. You have the right to remain silent. Anything you say can and may be held against you in a court of law. If you don't have an attorney, one will be appointed for you."

"Arrested?" Jay choked in disbelief. Over his shoulder as they cuffed him he demanded, "For what? What's the charge?"

"For the murder of Agent John Stover." Jay Dawson had no choice but to go with them. In the frozen silence of the room, as they marched passed the bar, Jay caught Mic's eye and held it all the way out the door.

*　*　*

At the police station, after Jay's lawyer arrived, the interview went relatively easy. It was as though they had already known the answers.

First, proper introductions were made.

"This is Sergeant Kozelle and I'm Lt. Marston. You're a difficult man to locate." Lt. Marston was all business.

"Mr. Dawson, we can skip the preliminary information such as name and address because we have that. But occupation, name of employer, that information we don't have so can you volunteer it?" The sergeant was too cordial in Jay's estimation.

"I'm a broadcasting engineer for ABS Broadcasting,"

"Engineer? How might that be a reason for our not being able to locate you too easily?" asked Marston.

"It's not exactly nine to five. I'm on call twenty-four hours a day. At three a.m. when a transmitter breaks down, I'm called to put it back to rights, sometimes I'll take the rest of the day off, if there is any left. Sometimes ten hours to repair one of those things is not unusual.

"This past week I was in another county erecting a 150-foot antenna and sleeping on site. I was the guest of a sister station, who wanted my technical expertise in installing the final step of their microwave system." Jay hoped he wouldn't have to go into any technical description.

"Hm, interesting. Do you know Amanda Shahey?" the sergeant changed the subject sharply.

"Yes."

"How?"

"She was a barmaid at McDougal's."

"Do you know each other socially?"

"Yeah. Once we went to the Rocks and once we went target shooting in the mountains, and no we were never intimate."

"What did you shoot for target practice?"

"Uh," Jay looked at his lawyer, and got the nod to answer. "A .44," Jay said.

"Mr. Dawson, this is the last question. Where were you on the morning of October 19th?"

"I went into the station early to catch up. I was dubbing my voice on commercials, and doing some mechanical repairs. Then about six I went to McDougal's for supper and stayed until closing."

"Mr. Dawson, please understand that we must keep you in jail until we check out your story."

Jay's lawyer did little to comfort him. "We can do nothing more here until they check out your story. They have your fingerprints on the murder weapon and you are the prime suspect. You are the only suspect in the vicinity and they have to put you in jail. I'll check out some of these ambiguities and get back with you in the morning."

No sleep came to Mr. Dawson while he was behind bars. His brain kept mulling over the events leading to his current position. "Damn, I knew I should have jumped from that truck!" Jay thought.

Almost twenty-four hours later, he was released for lack of evidence. Although his alibi checked out, his discharge came with a warning. "Please understand, Mr. Dawson, you are not under arrest, but if you must leave town for job related reasons, please notify the department before doing so. Thank you for your time here. You are free to go."

The sergeant got up from his desk and went into an adjoining office, and shut the door.

Jay felt totally disassociated from the events of his arrest, as though it had not really happened to him. He had remained calm. It wasn't until he got home that he fell apart. Heading for the fridge, he pulled out a beer. Reconsidering, he put it back. He got out a tumbler from the cupboard next to the fridge, then opening the good scotch someone had given him as a gift, he poured himself a triple.

"What the hell did they mean I am 'not under arrest, but...?' Shit, I know exactly what they meant!

"Good God Almighty, the 19th? A week later we went target shooting. For all I know I was the last person to handle that gun. Amanda had me return it to the glove box in her truck.

"Boy, Amanda sure can take care of herself, but I didn't know she was framing me. I'll bet it was that shooting she told me about. I should have jumped from that pickup when I had the chance.

"Now what do I do? Later. I'll think about this later. This scotch needs my undivided attention."

Having given the bottle his undivided attention, later it was. Jay woke up to the sound of his pager going off. Still dressed, he found himself on the floor with an empty bottle of scotch standing watch over him.

He phoned the station.

"Yeah, this is Dawson. What's up?"

"Transmitter on Paykin Hill has gone down. Get your ass over there and fix it," ordered the unsympathetic voice.

"Hey, be nice to me. I've had a bad night."

"I'll give you bad night. You haven't known bad until the station loses the 8 o'clock Sunday morning church service. Then you have to deal with every fricking righteous soul who phones wanting to know why they can't get Reverend Whoever on their TV sets."

"Okay, okay. I'm on my way."

Peering at his watch eased his mind, but not his hangover. There were four hours before the Reverend aired. Hopefully that would be enough time.

"Caffeine, caffeine. I need caffeine," chanted Jay as he arrived at the twenty-four hour donut shop. "If the alcohol doesn't kill me, the caffeine and cholesterol will. Ha," Jay continued talking to himself. "What a joke. The point is academic, especially if I get convicted of murder."

He knew worry was pointless. He shook it off and decided to concentrate on the task at hand. The repair was made by seven o'clock before the station signed on. "Yes!" Jay mimicked a cheer. "Dawson averts a march on the city by the panic-stricken homebound churchgoers!" He laughed at the incongruity of it all. But he knew his lawyers were working on reconciling the differences.

10

Painfully aware, was he, that his private moments would no longer be so private. President Thomas Glenelly loved to cultivate roses. Upon becoming president elect, the personal time that he spent alone amongst his prize winning specimens was gone. He learned that he could never be physically removed from his body guards.

The flowers, however, transported him to another world, and those close to him knew he couldn't be disturbed during his sessions in his garden. He took solace, comfort, therapy, whatever you wanted to call it, by digging into the dirt and putting some of his physical energy into his plants.

"This has got to cease," he thought. "I can't even take a leak without someone checking on me." One morning while he was in his greenhouse potting around, some of his energy went into planning to dodge the Secret Service.

He accidentally, on purpose, dropped his pruning shears onto the floor. "Oh, dear," he said while stooping to retrieve them. He left one gloved hand on the work surface. While he was beneath the level of the bench, he slipped out of his glove, leaving it on the bench, and dodged around to the other side of the table.

"Ha, ha," he laughed to himself. "Look at those guys getting all anxious. Uh, oh here they come, better resurface." Very nonchalantly he stood up, as though nothing was amiss, and instantly the Secret Service relaxed, but only just a bit, because they never relax when they're on duty.

"Once a day, I'm going to shake those guys," he committed to himself. Thomas Glenelly not only tried it once a day, he became very good at it. Once he was able to hide for a full three minutes. He left his bedroom at the White House and without being seen, doubled back. He sat, undetected for three minutes, then when he became bored, he reappeared in the hallway. He found the Secret Service frantic.

"Mr. Glenelly, where were you?"

"I was in my bedroom. You just saw me come out."

"Yes, but I saw you leave and go down the hall to your study. When did you return? How did you return?" They couldn't figure out where he had gone, or how he returned.

Thomas smiled. "I've got to keep you guys on your toes. You know, how Cato did for Inspector Clouseau?"

"With all due respect, Sir, that's not funny." Glenelly laughed and walked away. The Service held their heads, then held their eyes and ears open even wider. This president intended to give them fits.

Glenelly knew better than to try this in a foreign country, but while in the States, he felt it injected a bit of lightness into his otherwise serious day. It was a very upscale version of hide and seek.

"He's got a double. I swear it. How else did he dive into the ocean and then be on the beach a half mile away?"

That time in Destin, Florida, Glenelly wanted to see if he still had any of the old navy training still left in him.   He disappeared beneath the surface and swam until he thought his lungs would burst. When he came up for air, he could see the Service going nuts, so he disappeared again and when he came up he was a half-mile down the beach. They found him eating a hot dog and sucking down a Coca-Cola at a concession stand.   He was surrounded by school-age children.

Could a president really swim, go to the beach and eat junk food, just like them? They were all dumbstruck and excited at the importance of finding this man in their midst. The press was sworn to secrecy. If the world were to find out that President Thomas Glenelly was Clouseau's Cato, every crackpot would shadow him for just the right moment for the kill. His evasive tactics were not to be made public. This personality trait needed to be camouflaged.

The Destin Beach incident was billed as a human interest story for public relations. Should the question about the presence of security arise, they would admit to being there, only very difficult to see. Any negligence would be denied.

This half hour absence would be a hard record to break, and the head of Secret Service confronted the man.

"Mr. President, you've got to stop this. You're making my men crazy.   Be a good president and quit the shenanigans. The world is full of unfriendlies. They're everywhere. One of these days one of them is going to get you."

"If you guys can't keep up with me, what makes you think someone unfriendly will?"

There was something mad about the logic, and the Service couldn't convince Mr. Glenelly to behave as a proper public figure should.

The president had been out of sight from the Service for almost a half hour. Glenelly wondered if he could top that. He did. It was the end of the summer and there were some foreign dignitaries visiting the Midwest farm lands. They were in Iowa when President Glenelly slipped off between the rows of corn. Glenelly was gone for an hour. It was uncanny how the man knew when the focus wasn't on him and he could just slip away.

Thomas Glenelly grew up with corn. In Iowa, his father, and his father's father farmed corn. By the time Thomas was born, the farm had enough modern equipment and contract labor, that he never got involved with the day to day cultivation or harvesting of the grain.

He watched his father manage the accounts and the acreage. Then he went to college to learn law to help the agricultural industry. He was going to lobby for the farmers. Along the way, he foresaw that agriculture in the US was losing ground. Working hard lobbying, he didn't feel would be to much avail or profit. He learned more money was to be had in criminal law. After graduation Thomas Glenelly went to one of the law firms in Washington, DC. He helped draft the bylaws for arms control and made quite a name for himself as a prosecutor.

It's not that he forgot corn. It's just that he knew someone else was tending to it. Perhaps that was the reason he was so out of touch with the average citizen in the US. He figured someone else was tending to them. He knew the homeless existed as well as the poor, but he never came into contact with them.

International problems were so much more demanding. The Middle East was in a volatile situation. Cuba and Haiti had benevolent dictators, but dictators none the less. Korea was allying with Russia and there seemed to be a bed of coals glowing hotter and hotter each day. China's political situation was inflammable. The warlords were winning in the African countries despite civilization's attempt to overthrow them. Civil wars in the Eastern European block were constantly waging. America? America would take care of itself. Wasn't that the reason for all those agencies?

Out of touch was how most of America described Thomas Glenelly. His eyes were too far to the future, too far from the country. Would someone please hook him and reel him in? It was time he paid attention to domestic problems.

But the president was having fun dodging the helicopters running through the rows of corn as though he were a little kid. After an hour he emerged from the corn like, "What? Is there something wrong?" The Service organized themselves well enough to comb through the stalks, but not well enough to find him. He exited the rows just where he had entered them.

The Secret Service knew Glenelly was a challenge to protect, but they rose to the challenge by doubling his guard whenever he was outside the White House. There were already enough bells and whistles on the House itself. They weren't so much afraid of intrusion as they were the president just leaving and walking to another government building. They figured, unless he dug a tunnel or jumped over the fences, he wouldn't ever get by the guards at the gate.

Once he thought he could leave by smuggling himself out in his wife's car. Glenelly was slightly embarrassed when he was discovered climbing into the trunk of her car.

"No, Mr. President," the Secret Service man said. "We protect your wife as well as you, only she doesn't play games."

"One of these days I'm going to show you guys."

"Excuse me, Mr. President, but I think you have already shown us. Don't feel called upon to do it again." It almost sounded like he was being told off, but Glenelly shrugged, and let it pass. Then he went back to the more serious business of being a president.

11

"What the hell is this piece of shit?" asked the president irritated.

"Shit, Sir? I hardly think that this bill is shit."

"Well, that's your problem, Kershaw, you hardly ever think."

Judson Kershaw drew himself up, and took a deep breath. He was ready for a fight. This wasn't the first time that he, or any of his efforts had been insulted. From the very beginning of the presidential campaign, Glenelly never hid his true feelings when they were in private quarters. In public, however, Thomas Glenelly always wore his second face. Kershaw could always count on Glenelly's reaction to him: publicly praised, privately despised. The vice president was getting weary from the battering.

"Come on, Thomas, this is a very well executed bill. In fact, I used your pre-election platform to draw on it. How can you say it's shit?"

Glenelly sat back in his high backed chair. His elbows resting on the arms, he lifted his hands to his lips and made a small A-frame with the fingers and thumbs. "I can say it very easily, Judson. It was self-serving then, and it is self-serving now."

"What are you talking about? You addressed poverty and homelessness like a general taking command before you were elected. It was an admirable stance. What's changed?"

"The US changed, and it's a pity you're not changing with it."

"What?!"

"My economic advisors, if you would just listen to them, say the economy is not as dismal as the media would have us believe. I used that poverty platform to gain votes, and it worked."

"The fact that it worked should be proof enough that the American people believe there is a desperate concern with welfare and homelessness. Didn't you see last month's figures from the mortgage industry? Home repossessions are up sixty-three per cent, automobiles fifty per cent. You don't think there's an inherent problem? With all due respect, Mr. President, what you need is a whack up the side of the head."

"With all due respect, Mr. Vice President, fuck you. All you care about is that miserable black twenty per cent of the population your skin color represents."

"What's wrong with that? I owe-----"

"You owe nothing! Get realistic and off your high horse. There's another eighty per cent to this country that needs tending to."

"Thomas, you and I do not get along. That goes without saying. For once, would you please give me your own, uninterrupted by official advisors, opinion? How do you really see it? Coming off the campaign trail and seeing what you saw, and hearing the concerns that were spoken, what do you believe? What's your gut feeling? Pull off the blinders your advisors gave you, and what do you see?"

Judson Kershaw was speechifying, and Thomas Glenelly knew it. Kershaw was effective, that's how he made the ticket. Glenelly knew that, too. Kershaw was so effective, Glenelly could feel the blinders begin to peel away at the corners. The president could not understand the feeling of helplessness, or was it hopelessness? Whatever it was, he could not understand why this black man, whom he despised, all of a sudden stopped him dead in his tracks, and made him reexamine his motives, his position and indeed what he stood for. He sat frozen in confusion.

The vice president unaware of the impact he had just made on his political partner, thought he was being given the silent treatment. He grabbed the rough draft of the bill he had just presented for preliminary approval and stomped out of the Oval Office without a word. "This man has got to be gone! He has no business running a country," he resolved silently.

12

Just what was it that awakened Bob Gregg at three o'clock in the morning? He lay in his bed listening.

Usually a sound sleeper, he knew it had been something that had gotten the attention of his subconscious.
Brrrrng.
There it was, the phone. His wife answered it and handed it to him.

"Yeah," he blurted disgruntled at the ungodly hour of the disturbance.

"Gregg, Operations. What the hell took you so long?"

"Cut the crap. It's three-goddamn-o'clock in the morning. What's up?"

"There's been some vandalism at the Washington Monument. Get out there now before the tourists do."

"Right," he said hanging up.

Running his hands through his hair, Gregg vigorously rubbed his scalp in an attempt to get his brain to start. His system didn't really engage until seven o'clock, and then not until it was fueled with one cup of coffee.

He slipped into a pair of jeans and his leather jacket. Stopping in the kitchen, he boiled some water and brewed a cup of instant. Maybe he could quick jump his brain into action.

By three-thirty he was driving into DC, traffic free. In a few hours the freeway would be jammed with cars, all at a standstill.

Bob Gregg had been a ranger with the national parks for twenty-five years. In the early part of his career, the Defense Department recognized his keen mind. Gregg attributed it to those many hours of mindless guarding of government property. While on guard, his brain quickly processed situations needing solutions. His left-handed perspective of the world soon gave rise to answers.

A friend working in the Defense Department stopped by one day and casually mentioned how his day was going, off the record, of course. Within twenty-four hours, Gregg had worked out a few options to resolve the problem situation. The solution he recommended was the one implemented.

After helping to resolve three such situations, Gregg was screened by ATI (Antiterrorist Intelligence) and added to their unofficial list of authorized personnel. On the books he would always be a park ranger. In reality he served as an agent with Anti Terrorist Intelligence (ATI). As an agent he paid for himself three times over during his tenure as a park ranger.

Over the years he had generally enjoyed his job and the rise to a position of responsibility. In the last five years, though, his zeal had left him. In six months, he would be retiring and he looked forward to the rest.

He perceived a public disrespect for property, especially historical. He had done what he could to increase the nation's awareness and appreciation for classic architecture.

He did this through the local television station with the help of a broadcast engineer, Jay Dawson. Together they made a documentary of some of the national monuments and other classic architecture in America, including the Washington Monument, the tallest masonry structure in the world.

The Public Broadcasting System had seen it and aired it on their network. The result? More vandalism. Bob Gregg figured the vandals probably never watched PBS. What the hell, he thought, he had tried.

He cursed every time he saw a building being torn down to make way for the latest architectural atrocity. There was no appreciation for the quality of classic lines in this country.

Whether the building was there for more than 100 years or less than ten, it was demolished to make way for a structure that could get more revenues for the property owners.

Setting his pet peeve aside, he parked curbside at the monument. He joined the three other rangers waiting for him at the base of the monument.

One of the men he used to work with before he moved to ATI approached him. "Hey, Gregg. How you doing? What, no tie?" he asked trying to break the ice.

"I have a strict dress code. Don't wear ties this early in the day." Bob Gregg shot his old associate a smile. "Ungodly hours call for comfort, not class. Now, what's the situation here?" The junior ranger, who had discovered the vandalism, was impressed by Gregg's position and he began his dissertation.

"I came on duty at 23:00 hours, replacing Douglass. At that time when I made the rounds there was nothing-----"

"Son?"

"Yes, Sir?"

"Cut the bullshit and give me the short version."

"Yes, Sir. I was making my rounds this last time and as I approached the monument, there was this illusion that the top of the monument was broken. That's when I radioed the office."

"Well, let's go see what this looks like, gentlemen," the senior ranger suggested.

"I don't know what it is, Sir, but it looks like something is covering it," offered the young ranger.

All of them stared. Flood lights from the ground illuminated the light stone. The early morning sky offered deep indigo as a back drop. Something darker, something black, was obscuring the top of the structure. It wasn't very big.

Gregg looked around him. Lighted DC was sparkling. He looked toward the White House. It seemed peaceful. The Mall seemed peaceful. This monument was peaceful except for this thing hanging on it.

He muttered his curse to the disrespectful public and turned to look at the other rangers.

"What time did the monument close yesterday?"

"17:00, Sir."

"Anything worth noting while you were on duty?"

"No sir. I didn't even hear anything hit, Sir."

"Hit? Why would you say "hit"?"

"Well, Sir, I sort of imagine a catapult somewhere and----"

"Yeah, I see. Interesting." Gregg looked at the top again. Scratching his head vigorously, he asked, "What is it? How did it get there? I thought the college fraternities were finished with their hell week."

"We're going to need a crane to get it down," one of the rangers said.

"Vandals are getting too sophisticated these days," Gregg observed. Another reason he was looking forward to retirement. He turned to address his men. "It's the only thing that makes sense at the moment, so until we have something further to go on, check for evidence of any mechanical device that could uh, eh, let's say catapult something this high."

It was not permissible to navigate the sky in these parts of DC, so he ruled out dropping out of the sky, jettisoned from an aircraft. He would check with air traffic control as well as the Secret Service's own radar system. Since the crash of the Cessna into the White House in 1994, additional radar and missile ordnance was placed on top of certain government buildings.

He wondered if the bag could have been applied internally. Too many questions, too early, for someone too old, Gregg shook his head. This one was going to take some thought and some help. Maybe some gang or group would own up to it and he wouldn't have to devise a theory.

As Bob Gregg left the monument he had the gut feeling that this was no ordinary vandalism. He ordered the object to be removed and brought to his office. "Treat it like evidence," he ordered.

If he were lucky, maybe a catapult would be found.

Looking toward the White House before leaving, Gregg muttered, "Wouldn't it be nice to live in a big white house and not have to worry about traffic jams or stupid vandals?"

"Pardon me, Sir?"

"Sorry, just thinking aloud."

Gregg knew the president had more important things on his mind than traffic gridlocks and more hazardous people in his life than vandals, but for once Gregg wished he could leave the pettiness of life to someone else.

There was no need to close the monument since there was no apparent danger. He was glad he wasn't in Operations. They were the ones who were going to have to get the crane to remove the blasted sack.

As he walked back to his car, he roused, "Come on, retirement!"

13

Michael Chessie pointed his white van into the traffic and drove away from the Washington Monument. The test flight conducted on the monument was a complete success. They had hung back to watch the reaction if there was any to the one glitch in their trial flight. They watched the meeting of the rangers as they discussed the bag atop the monument.

"What do you think, Killian?" asked Chessie.

"The hang glider handles beautifully. A real melding of art and science, that one. We were undetected from release to landing. We even got by the increased radar. Everything is working. We have the schedule for the ranger patrols. At that time of the morning, no one can hear or see us coming. It was perfect except for that one unexpected pocket in the air current."

"What did happen, exactly? Why did you drop the sandbag?" Chessie wanted to get it clear in his mind.

"I hit a pocket of cold air," reasoned Killian, "And the hang glider began to drop. The only thing for me to do to get the distance I wanted, was to drop the ballast, or pseudo launcher, if you will."

"Well, no one saw us or heard it hit. By the time anyone figures out how it happened, it will be too late," nodded Chessie in approval. The experiment which was successful this morning helped to solidify their timing and confirm their plans.

"Security's reaction time was faster than I expected. I didn't believe they would be that thorough. When are you scheduled to get the explosives?" asked Killian.

"I'm meeting a sergeant outside Quantico Marine Base this afternoon. I'll be getting them then."

"What's Frank going to be doing?"

"While I'm at Quantico, and you're headed back to the Skyline, I'll have Frank take the plane up and circle the orchards. After all, I've got to do something to substantiate the story that we're scientists studying the effects of acid rain."

"Some humanitarians we are," Killian commented wryly.

"Yeah, we're in the right place for that story," smiled Chessie.

The two compatriots turned northwest on Route 7 towards Leesburg. There Chessie had bought a vacant farm under the guise of scientific research. He and his team were to be studying the effects of acid rain on fruit orchards. At first they met with some resistance, but when they hit on the emotional cord of acid rain the team was welcomed with open arms. It was emotional because of nearby Mount Mitchell, and its balsam trees.

Because of the attached emotional connotation there was support. Chessie laughed at how well this fit into the plan.

After dropping Killian at the farm in Leesburg, Chessie pointed the van toward Interstate 66. He knew he had an hour's ride ahead of him before reaching the marine base in Quantico, Virginia.

Mentally he went over his check list: $125,000 cash, a stuff sack, a blanket, and a token thank you gift, all in the rear of the van. His 9mm automatic was on the passenger seat next to him. He exited Interstate 95 onto Route 1 which would bring him closer to Quantico. As he neared the base, he recognized the quonset hut bar, which had been described to him for this particular transaction. The bar had been closed for a very long time. The run down piece of military metal was on a triangular point of property bordered on one side by a secondary road, and a dirt road on the other. The pie shaped lot was gravel and spotted with two-foot growth of weeds. Access to the parking lot in the rear of the hut was available from either side.

This establishment was in the middle of nowhere, perhaps the reason for its demise. Chessie pulled into the parking lot and waited for the sergeant. He was not happy at all with the meeting arrangements. He was accustomed to conducting his business in areas which could afford more privacy. True, this place was nowhere, but this parking lot could be observed from both roads. He would have to trust the sergeant.

"Ah, well," he thought, his Belfast instincts activated, "I shall have to conduct myself accordingly. I do hope the sergeant has exercised good judgment."

His wait was not long. The designated blue Pontiac Grand-Am pulled in beside him. As Chessie prepared to exit the van, he stuck the 9mm gun into his belt at his back, beneath his jacket.

"Mr. Chess?" asked the woman getting out of the driver's seat of the Grand Am.

"What the devil is this?" demanded Chessie. "First you decide to make this transaction in a bloody fish bowl, now I find it's a woman making the delivery. Can nothing go right?"

"Stop the macho bullshit, and let's get on with it," the sergeant stated irritably. With that she walked toward the rear of her car and opened the trunk. "I presume you have the agreed upon sum?" she asked a bit too smugly.

"I have the agreed upon sum if you have the goods," he replied.

"I went through a lot of trouble to secure these missiles. You're aware that they are state of the art?"

"Thank you for the lecture, my good woman, but it isn't necessary. I'm happy to see that the greatest military power in the world has finally come abreast with progress."

"You're getting a bargain for 150 G's," mentioned the sergeant beginning to transfer the goods.

Chessie took a deep breath. He expected something like this to occur and came prepared. "The agreed upon sum was $125,000 not $150,000."

"Well, as it turns out, my expenses ran a little higher than I first estimated, so I had to adjust the price. You know how it is."

"Yah, I know how it is," he said not showing any of the annoyance that he felt. "To tell you the truth, I expected the price to go up even more than $25,000 so I came prepared." Walking to the rear of the van, Chessie opened one of the doors and reached in and grabbed the stuff sack. He walked back. Just before he got to her he let the bag drop to the ground. When he squatted to retrieve the sack with his left hand, the woman was momentarily distracted, and did not see him pull his pistol with the right. He picked up the sack and lunged at the woman with the sack and the gun between them. Startled by the quick action, the woman was nearly knocked over. It came too quickly for her to react. Pressing the sack and pistol to the woman's chest, he pulled the trigger.

There was no time for fear to register as the woman's wide eyed look of surprise took in Chessie. The shot was muffled due to the closeness of their bodies and the sack that came between them.

Chessie held her close to keep the body from collapsing, and walked her to the driver's side of the Grand Am. He put her behind the steering wheel.

"So sorry, Sergeant, but a fair price is a fair price. You know how it is." Quickly, Chessie exchanged the weapons crate with a token gift of gratitude.

As he got in to drive away, Chessie glanced back at the soldier in the car. Her head was skewed to the side. Except for the patch of crimson spreading on her shirt, the scene may have been reminiscent of the more active days of the ghost bar, as someone sat passed out at the wheel of their car. The van pulled away from the parking lot at a very prudent speed. The sergeant had made a good choice for rendezvous after all. Not one vehicle had passed the quonset hut during the transaction, and no one was encountered as Chessie made his getaway.

Five minutes later, Chessie heard a very loud explosion. He had been listening for it. "Thank you very much, Madam," he said to himself.

14

Driving carefully, Chessie arrived back at the Leesburg farm house with his cherished cargo. Had any traffic mishap occurred, he would have had trouble explaining the blood on his chest, particularly since it was not his.

Chessie backed the van up to one of the out buildings. He climbed between the seats and walked back to release the inside latch for the double doors.

Frank, his right hand man on the farm and confidante, had seen him arrive. He drove out to meet him. He reached the building just a few seconds after Chessie. Jumping out he went to the rear of the van to help with the doors. He pulled them completely open, and there was Chessie, hunched over, complete with blood stain on his shirt. Frank jumped forward to try and help as he thought Chessie had been wounded.

"My God, you've been hit!"

"I'm fine."

"What's happened? You're sure you are fine?"

"Everything is in perfect working order. Not so for our dear Sergeant. In fact she will not be needing this box with the $125,000."

"Box? Then what's this bag with the hole in it. Chessie, a gun's been shot through this."

"Look inside. I believe you'll be pleased to discover the remains of some very blank, but very well used blocks of note paper." He then recounted the turn of events as they carried the crate into the building.

"Genius. Absolute Genius. How did you know it would go that way?"

"It's my hawk's eye, remember?"

"Glad you handled those details. Now here are my details for the next couple hours." Frank delivered his edict. "I'll get the van washed, while you prepare the bonfire for that bloody shirt and sack of pretend money. Don't forget to----"

"Yes, Frank, I won't forget to scrub behind my ears. Just get on with it, for the love of St. Pete."

Frank grinned at the affectionate rebuff. His years of mothering Chessie always produced the same affect. It came as a natural progression of Chessie's caring for Frank after he had been saved from a South Carolina lynch mob disguised in the costume of the Ku Klux Klan. His mind wandered back to that event.

Chessie had been hunting on an estate in South Carolina one winter. It was early evening and already dark. As he and his horse came into a clearing in the woods, about a mile from the main house, the sight before him was frightening even though he knew bloodshed in his home country, Ireland.

A circle of men dressed in the garb of the KKK surrounded a burning cross. Next to the cross was a black man on his knees with his hands tied behind his back. The black man was Frank. Each member of the circle began taking turns kicking him. Two of the costumed men were closer to the woods beside a rope hanging from a tree limb.

Chessie rode up to the circle. "Looks like there's going to be some blood shed tonight." The circle of men laughed and began passing a bottle of whiskey, and the kicking continued. Something in Chessie snapped. He aimed his rifle at the base of the burning cross and shot. The flaming wood fell to the ground. Very quietly, he said, "The next one to kick that man won't have a foot to remember the experience." Out of defiance, the largest ghost kicked the black man. Chessie aimed and shot the assailants foot.

"You shot me you bastard!" the wounded man screamed.

"What a pity your hearing isn't any better. I won't hesitate to shoot again. Who's next?" Chessie saw the circle grow wider. He aimed at the rope hanging from the tree and shot it down. Half the men ran to the woods.
The other half tended to their shot comrade in crime and carried him screaming and moaning in the same direction the running group took.

Chessie got down from his horse and helped the black man. "Thank you," he said. "They were going to kill me."

"What had you done?" asked Chessie looking after the cuts on the man's face. "It ain't what I done. It's what I am."

"Yes," sighed Chessie. "Where I come from, we have a similar problem." Chessie let the man ride his horse back to the house. There they made introductions and bodily repairs. Frank swore allegiance to the Irishman and had been Chessie's right hand man ever since.

Frank smiled at the rebuff and the mention of St. Peter, and his mind returned to the task at hand: washing the van. After the bonfire, Chessie returned to the outbuilding to find

Frank pouring two cups of coffee. Silently they picked up the cups and walked to the back wall of the building. Pressing a special place below the rakes and shovels, a small portion of the wall slid open. The opening revealed a long, narrow corridor that resembled a war room. There were timetables tacked to the walls, and maps carefully highlighted covered the two-by-fours providing the infrastructure of the building. Log books and check lists were carefully maintained on a makeshift desk of a door lying horizontally on two small file cabinets whose drawers could barely fully open for the confining walls.

"Has Killian left?"

"No, he's asleep. He intends to leave this evening."

"Good, we're moving on schedule," announced Chessie, ticking off the last known movements of Shahey and Killian. "But damn that phone call from Shahey. If only she hadn't killed that agent. That one event has created the necessity to complete the operation in a few days, rather than two months. We needed that time."

"So, why are you concerned? You've had to move quickly before. After changing the timetable, nothing has ever gone wrong," reminded Frank.

"Yes, but we were on our own turf in Ireland where there's a war in the streets. Must I remind you we are in the United States of America, especially in the District of Columbia, where for those who organize, organization is an obsession? Where red tape and bureaucratic palaver has every cubic inch of atmosphere watched by some clerical twit? We have got to be more brilliant in our ideas, more intellectual in our approach, more knowing where human frailty enters the picture, and we also need more than our share of good luck."

"And always in memorial to those who have gone before us needlessly," interjected Frank lifting his mug in a toast.

"Indeed. Needlessly," whispered Chessie alluding to their families, and he, too, lifted his mug.

15

He was a man driven by self imposed deadlines. Even his leisure moments had to be orchestrated to perfection. Tonight he was to be at Campground 7 off Sky Line Drive in the Shenandoah Mountains. Eric Killian pulled in just before midnight, driving from Chessie's farm in Leesburg.

Even if he hadn't been there by midnight, it wouldn't have mattered, but he liked to keep in practice on or off an assignment. He took pride in perfection.

His arrival was made in total darkness. Everyone else in the campground was asleep within their tents. If the stars had been illuminated, he would have erected a tent, but on this moonless night, Eric just stared back at the pinpoints and took a sleeping bag from the back of the four wheel drive. Unrolling it on the ground, he crawled in and went to sleep.

It was six o'clock a.m. when Killian felt someone shaking him. On impulse he reached under his head. His hand came to rest calmly on a piece of steel as he saw that it was a park ranger who had wakened him, a female park ranger.

"This your vehicle?"

"Yes."

"You're not registered," she drawled in her most authoritative voice.

"I arrived rather late last evening, darlin', and didn't have the pleasure," he said in his most beguiling Irish voice.

"What time was that?"

"Nearly midnight," he offered, making it look like he was using his arm to bolster his head, but not moving from his sack.

"You're sleeping in a common area rather than a designated camp sight. We don't allow that."

"Considering the lateness of the hour and the depth of the darkness, it was difficult to tell one area from another." How long was he going to have to parry with this bitch? He had to get rid of her. "Look, I'm sorry for the oversight. I promise to come to the office to register."

"That'll be alright, then." She eyed Killian thinking what a milquetoast he was lying there, not jumping to attention in her presence. "Where you from, England?"

"Close. Ireland."

"Irish? Did you turn left at the Blarney Stone or something? And what's that long bundle on top of your Trooper?" Her tone of authority was giving way to one of animosity since he wasn't getting up.

"It's a hang glider."

"A hang glider!" the ranger exclaimed in disbelief. She looked at the twenty foot bundle on top of the Isuzu, then down at Killian. The animosity was replaced by curiosity. How could this red haired, fair skinned wimp do anything so dangerous as hang glide?

As the ranger turned and looked fully at the roof of the Trooper, Killian took the opportunity to conceal the gun and get out of the sleeping bag.

"Let's have it," said the ranger.

"I beg your pardon?" Killian spoke poker faced but his adrenaline began to pump.

"Yeah, what gives? You're a long way from home. What's the reason you're in this country? Let's have it."

"The reason?" his heart rate began to decrease. "The reason is that I have heard so much about the American hang gliding experience that I wanted to try for myself."

"When you register," the ranger said smiling, "we'll discuss some primo launch sites."

"Thank you very much, but I've brought some topographical maps of the valley that should enable me to find them without troubling you," Killian tried to beg off politely.

"No problem. My pleasure, in fact. You see there are some areas that are rather secluded and the only access is by fire trail or no trail at all. I'll see you at the office," she said walking away. "Nice body," she thought. "Maybe he has balls after all."

"Shit," thought Killian, "this isn't what I need." He began punching the sleeping bag into its stuff sack, threw it into the back of the Isuzu, holstered the gun, and concealed it beneath the camping equipment. After slamming the back door, he drove to the camp store. There he took a quick shower and prepared himself mentally for the tedious task of registration.

The ranger station was a short walk from the store, so he left his truck parked. He entered the office calmly although he was seething inwardly.

"Hello there, Irish. You know, we never introduced ourselves," the ranger said smiling. "I'm Susan Safran. Folks around here call me Ranger Sue."

"Right, I'm Killian, Eric Killian. Where are these registration forms?"

"The papers are ready, and here are maps with the more accessible launch sites. You can try those today. Since I have the next two days off, I can accompany you to the more isolated ones. Think of me as your personal tour guide while you're in this national park."

"Thank you, but it isn't necessary for you to go through all this trouble-----"

"No trouble. I'll meet you a little past six at your tent this evening, and we can discuss tomorrow's arrangements." Killian could see that Ranger Sue would not be an easy person to avoid, so he acquiesced.

"See you at six then," he said putting his signature on the registration papers. As Killian left the station, he smiled to himself and thought, "This might work out better than expected. What could be more helpful to a terrorist than to be under the watchful eye and guiding hand of a park ranger? As long as this Ranger Sue thinks she is orchestrating each of our meetings, I should come to no harm in the park. Any other ranger questioning my presence will be disarmed by her presence or by the mention of her name. A quick radio check would verify any of my claims."

Killian was looking forward to meeting this Sue later in the day. "A personal tour guide might not be such a bad idea," he thought as he headed the truck toward his first launch site.

16

Autumn in the Shenandoah contains colors that the artist always tries to duplicate on palette and canvas. Nature and the mind remember from year to year how it's done, but each recurring season seems to be more breathtaking than the last.

The people who play with the elements, as those who hang glide, get above the trees and fields and feel the color rise to envelop them along with the smells of a coming winter and the lifts of air. The sport seems to temporarily free you from any of earth's influences, and some truly feel connected to the universe.

Eric Killian had a super second day hang gliding. The new state of the art craft gave him no trouble. He and his craft were one. Whoever had designed this fourth generation model was a genius. He would have to congratulate them.

It was nearly six o'clock when Killian had built a fire in the designated fire ring for his camp site. After all he would not want to get into trouble with the rangers for something so elementary.

Enjoying the fire and his sips of red wine, he sat reviewing his topographical maps. He had circled six possible launch points within close proximity of the camp site. He didn't want to wander too far, as he had to be in Leesburg in three days.

As he studied the maps, he could hear Ranger Sue approaching quietly from behind him. "What do you think of these sites I've chosen?" he asked her as soon as she was within earshot.

"How could you hear me coming?" she asked in amazement. "I was being as quiet as I possibly could!"

"Obviously, you weren't quiet enough," Killian said casually. Over his shoulder she saw the sites he had chosen.

"That's amazing!" she exclaimed. "Those six points include four of the ones I was going to suggest." She didn't know what to make of this red headed man. "Irish, your looks are deceiving."

"How's that?"

"You don't look that good or that clever. How'd you figure all this?"

"I'm an expert," he beamed his best smile up at her.

"Okay, hotshot, if you're so smart, are you aware that alcoholic beverages are prohibited in national parks?" she asked spying his glass of wine.

"Uh, no."

"All right then---where's my glass?"

Killian removed a second wine goblet from the bag at his feet, relieved she was participating in the infraction. He then poured her a glass of wine. Safran studied the map further while she drank. Killian started the steaks.

"I'll assume you'll stay for supper?" asked Killian.

"Hmm," she responded holding her glass of wine out in front of her to inspect it. "Those steaks just might make a right good accompaniment for this wine. Something I just couldn't, in my right mind, pass up. You assume correctly, Mr. Killian, I will be staying for dinner."

"Great, now what about the other two sites that you hadn't suggested?"

"I know where they are. They could be quite difficult to get to due to their limited access."

"What difficulties need to be overcome?"

"We'd have to park the vehicle and hike in. One hike would be about a mile and a half."

"Excuse me. Did you say 'we'?"

"If you want to get to them, it's 'we'," instructed Ranger Sue.

"All right, then, 'we' will leave those to the end."

After dinner and finishing the wine, Ranger Sue excused herself and left for her cabin. Eric Killian was glad to see her leave. Her dissertations on the outdoor life and roughing it were too much for his ears to bear. He'd met other knowledgeable women in his life, but they had the good sense not to bore him with the details. If he could get past the talk, the clumsy climbing boots, and dumpy ranger clothing, he was sure he'd find something there more to his liking.

Killian took one last look at his map, drained his glass, turned off the lantern and went to bed.

Next morning, Ranger Sue arrived punctually. "Good morning, Irish," she said helping herself to a cup of coffee.

"Top of the mornin' to ya, Ranger Sue," Killian said jovially, finishing his coffee. "Are you ready?"

"Yes. The closest site is near Loft Mountain," the ranger said as the two got into the Isuzu. "It's five miles ahead on the right. Just past the drive into the overlook is a fire trail. Turn there."

Ranger Sue had always been awed by the panoramic view from Sky Line Drive, and she wasn't going to neglect telling the man from Ireland all about it.

Killian didn't listen to half her banter. He caught bits and pieces, "...today is an unusual day...haze usually...clear views down into the valleys..." and wished she would just shut up.

Ranger Sue as usual forgot herself for a moment and got on her soap box about encroaching development and the effect it was having on the Blue Ridge.

"You always this quiet, Irish? But I guess I haven't given you much chance to speak. What's Ireland look like?"

"Very beautiful," he said trying to get away with saying as little as possible. He wanted her to be quiet, but he didn't want to antagonize her either, so he continued. "This reminds me a little of Ireland. We have beautiful rolling hills to the south, and it is very green in the country. In summer the hills are covered with----"

"Turn here. This is the fire trail."

17

There are domestic terrorists: domestic, as in family, those that terrorize their own families and by extension of fear, their neighbors. There are national terrorists: fanatics who take legitimate national issues, like "rights to life," animal welfare and minority causes, to fanatic extremes of violence. And then---then there are international terrorists.

They all have similar psychological profiles, but the latter have greater needs. They need a cause that stretches beyond international boundaries. They need friends, cloaked friends, near the levels of power, and above all, they need money.

Secretary of State Blankenship, learned many years ago that one man's trash is another's treasure. As secretary and team player, Blankenship publicly supported the current administration in its efforts to combat terrorism regardless of origin. Privately, Blankenship supported only himself.

Blankenship and Chessie had much in common. Both their fathers were pilots in WWII. Where Chessie actually owned and flew the vintage craft, Blankenship appreciated it. The two men met at a Paris air show several years ago. Both were admiring the aircraft. Blankenship was a spectator and Chessie was a buyer, adding a plane or two to his collection.

Over the years, the two men saw each other at other air shows and periodically had the odd dinner together. Chessie, carefully monitoring Blankenship's brilliant career through the bureaucratic ranks, aware of the potential return on his investment, went so far as to issue Blankenship an open invitation to his Virginia farm, where he could come and admire the collection he had, as well as take an occasional flight.

The two men began flying together. Chessie discovered that greed and personal gain motivated Blankenship, not personal commitment or loyalty.

After some time, Chessie began to allude to future international happenings and provided Blankenship with hints of possible money making avenues. The first or second time Chessie passed a tip Blankenship did nothing. But as Blankenship began to see events unfold as Chessie described, he could no longer resist the opportunity to increase his bankroll. He saw that Chessie was very well connected in world government although seemingly apolitical.

The closer Blankenship got to Chessie the more he began to suspect Chessie's connections. The relationship had now progressed to the point where it was like two drug junkies taking care of one another. Blankenship received his fix from Chessie in the form of enhanced investments and increased personal wealth. Chessie received his fix from Blankenship in the form of information. By this time both men were in bed with each other so deeply the only pathway of escape was death.

As Blankenship moved up in the State Department, he became the subject of Senate approval hearings. The method by which he had gained his fortune was often raised. He admitted to nothing but exceptionally good business sense and exposed no one.

As his success continued it became necessary for him to place his investments into a blind trust. The Watergate era of the '70s made it stylish for wealthy statesmen under the guise of propriety to divest themselves of day to day management of their personal wealth. This single act, in the public's eye, reduced the probability of conflict of interest. Who better to oversee his trust than the internationally successful businessman, Michael Chessie.

Chessie first approached Blankenship with the assassination scheme in the week following Chessie's dinner with the prime minister in London. Caution had to be exercised when approaching the subject. Bending the rules and making money is one thing, conspiring to kill the president of the United States is quite another. Was the conspiratorial relationship deep enough to allow this discussion?

Blankenship knew there was no way for himself to directly ascend to the presidency from a secretarial position. Kershaw was his recommendation to then presidential candidate Glenelly. Kershaw was Blankenship's pawn. During the years in office, Blankenship found he could mold and direct Kershaw as he needed.

By disposing of the president, he could be the proverbial power behind the throne. Put Kershaw in office, have himself nominated as vice president, then twist Kershaw further for personal gain.

The subject addressed, Blankenship's and Chessie's relationship deepened. They were bound by the only existing exit.

18

First the Berlin Wall was torn down in 1990.
Then
Gorbachov gave each of the Soviet States their freedom. The people of peace sighed and beheld in awe, the wonderment, the significance of the changing times, and thanked the powers that be for the enlightenment and evolvement of the species.

The people of subterfuge, espionage and terrorism worldwide, screamed a resounding NEVER! While holding their hands to the sky, they asked, "Now what do we do?" It didn't take long for the unenlightened and the unevolved to reactivate.

It was in the international briefings, where Blankenship testified in closed hearings held by the Senate Committee for the State of the World, that he always had to be careful with what he said.

"So, Mr. Blankenship, what good is all this freedom America seems to want so desperately for the rest of the world to participate in?   Look at what happened in the Balkans.   Escaping from under the thumb of Big Brother, they're all like sitting ducks midst a civil war with religious overtones.   I'd say they were better off under a dictatorship than what they've got now."

"Mr. Powell, you must never once think that.   We must be sure all their reforms succeed.   Democracy will be won or lost by the Russians themselves, but we must do all in our power to ensure that democracy does not fail.

"Allowing democracy to get a foothold in the Russian States and in Eastern Europe is the best possible scenario for military security in the West,"   explained Darian Blankenship.

"And what of the cold shoulder we received from Russia when NATO allowed Eastern Europe to join its ranks? Can you address that, Mr. Blankenship?"

"I have never claimed to understand the Russians. It's true that I was the internal expert at the State Department. I was even instrumental in calming the waters between Yeltsin and the hard-line communists, but that doesn't mean I understand them. I only worked with them to an effective end.

"Who knows?   Maybe they substituted Kremlin craziness for international insanity.   Perhaps they were making a statement of their own when the structural statement in East Berlin was razed," Blankenship studied the papers in front of him.

The committee had convened many times discussing Russia's reaction to Eastern Europe. "What posture do you feel we should take regarding the upcoming meeting in Budapest between the Russian Bears and the Hungarian Gyp-sies?"

"First of all, rid ourselves of the notion that we are dealing with bears and gypsies. We are dealing with nations of peoples that are driven by needs. Once those needs are met, we can meet them on common ground with mutual respect.

They believe in themselves, but we must believe in them, too. Many feel that they need arms to help protect their beliefs. Much depends on whether we share that belief."

Blankenship knew that most men were driven by greed. In his diplomatic position, he always played to this driving force in his opponent's unconscious. In so doing he could turn the opposition to his advantage and walk away with both sides victorious.

In no way could he reveal that he was in favor of issuing weaponry. If he would show his hand, he would write his own condemnation. Better to plant the seed, let them cultivate it, so he could reap the benefits of an innocent bystander who was secretly and highly vested in an ordnance portfolio.

The committee began to deliberate on what Blankenship had presented to them. As they droned on, the secretary of state made an effort to study his papers. He reflected on the rise to his current position.

When Thomas Glenelly was running for president, one of his advisors had mentioned Blankenship's name to him. Glenelly was most impressed with his win/win track record, and his mastery of diplomatic situations. Glenelly was not concerned with the man's methods, just his results, and he knew he wanted him as his secretary of state. So it was that in 1996, Mr. Darian Blankenship was appointed to that cabinet post.

By 1998, Blankenship had established himself as a man of tact and resolved action. He always got his way. More often than not his unremitting patience wore the opposition away. He held hands and stroked brows with the best of them, but in the end, he had appealed to their inner sense of reason, usually their greed, and they both came away winners.

Halfway through Glenelly's term, Darian Blankenship stepped out of character. He became impatient. Being well respected was not gaining him anything tangible. Very aware of the NEVER! that screamed through the subterranean universe in 1990, he knew that there were many men with a great deal of expertise underemployed above and below the hallowed halls of government throughout the world. Blankenship devised a plan.

Enlisting the help of the CIA, KGB and PLO, he would prove to the world leaders that these agencies were still very much in demand. Not at all outdated, but very much in sync with the ideologies of people they saved. Government subversion by the very agencies that swore protection to their individual governments would be deployed once again for peace keeping missions. Of course this would have to be done with guns. By design, with all the pacts that established it as a clearing house for weapons, America didn't need to build concessions between countries.

Contracts were signed. Blankenship's motto became "Go buy American to get by America."

If an investigator knew where to look for a most lucrative stock portfolio he would find a conflict of interest for the secretary of state of the United States. The paperwork would be more than incriminating. It overstepped lines of propriety and smacked of treason and treachery.

Mr. Blankenship was a very clever man. He made sure he left no tracks.

19

After Jay had restored the TV station's transmission of the Sunday morning service, he returned home and puttered around the bungalow he rented. He even worked on his pocket radar a little.

The next day, he phoned his lawyers. Nothing else had developed. They knew everything Jay knew to date, nothing more. They advised him to relax.

He went into work and tried to maintain business as usual. It was an antiquated station in a medium- sized market, not a bad stepping stone to a major network. Dawson moved from a small town in Colorado to a larger town in Virginia, south of Washington DC. His sights were set on the stations in the nation's capital. All he needed was a bit of luck and some good timing.

"What an unbelievable break," thought Jay throwing himself onto the sofa in his office. "If all goes well, maybe I can broadcast from inside a state prison, address: Death Row." He was mulling over the events of the weekend and was still convinced he would be found guilty of a crime he didn't commit.

He was startled back to reality when the secretary appeared in the doorway.

"Morning, Jay. Before work this morning, a Bob Gregg called. Said it was urgent that you phone him as soon as possible."

"Thanks. Give me the number. I'll phone him now," Jay said struggling to his feet. "Bob Gregg, that's a name I haven't thought of in months. I wonder what he wants."

At his desk, Jay dialed the familiar DC 202 area code.

"Gregg," the voice at the other end of the phone said curtly.

"Hey, Bob. It's Jay. What's up?"

"What in the world have you gotten yourself involved in there, son?" Gregg asked recognizing the voice.

Despite his bureaucratic position, Bob Gregg maintained a Southern demeanor with his friends. Jay smiled. He could almost imagine Bob, cigar in hand, in a rocking chair on his veranda beneath the shade of a great magnolia tree. He could almost hear Scarlet whispering in the background.

"What do you know and how do you know it?" Jay began cautiously.

"I saw a departmental message come across my desk stating that a certain Jay Dawson was arrested regarding the killing of an FBI agent. Would you like to fill me in on the details?"

Jay recapped the story quickly, and mentioned he had the services of a good and reputable lawyer.

"I don't know all the particulars, my good man, but I would not be breaking any confidences if I tell you that agent was hot on the trail of some CCPU operatives. Apparently he got close to getting one but they got him instead."

"CCPU? What's that?"

"Command Council for Protestant Ulster."

"Ulster? Isn't that the opposite of the IRA? They're the ones who want Northern Ireland to remain part of England."

"That's right."

"What exactly are they liberating?"

"Themselves. They don't want to be part of the Irish Republic because historically they owe their allegiance to the Crown. If they can remove the presence of both the IRA and the Royal Army, life should go on peacefully."

"Wouldn't it be easier if they just unified with the Republic?"

"You know the Irish. They never give up. You ever hear of the Israelis and the Palestinians? How about Bosnia? Well it's as easy as that."

"Civil war? Really?"

"Make no mistake. There would be just as much emotion and religious animosity as the conflicts in the early '90s.

"Great Britain seems more civilized than that."

"When people allow their passions to rule, there is no telling what disguise civilization will take. Don't forget, Sarejevo was where the 1990 Olympics were held. A beautiful city, Yugoslavia was best known to the world as a playground. People went there for seaside holidays and skiing vacations. That's one playground turned warground. No one goes there anymore unless they want to vacation in hell."

"Not to change the subject, but I told the police everything I know. I don't think they believed me."

"Don't sweat it, Jay. You didn't tell them anything they didn't already know. You were just reinforcing their prejudices, so to speak. Now they know what I've just told you, so they aren't interested in you. There are bigger, badder bastards to catch, and they know that, too."

"Bob, I appreciate your calling to tell me this, but the pressure won't be off until I don't have to tell the police about my out-of-town movements."

"Know what you mean, son. In the meantime, don't be such a stranger."

"I'll buzz ya' when I'm off the hook." Jay hung up the phone and picked up his pocket radar that was lying on his desk. Playing with it as he leaned back in his chair. CCPU operatives?! Terrorists is what he means. What the hell, is Amanda a terrorist? God, what a perfect cover. Add that to the never ending list of inconsistencies!

"You playing with that gadget again?" teased the station manager interrupting Jay's train of thought.

"Yeah, don't know who would ever need this, but it was fun putting it together."

"Number 19 has some routine maintenance scheduled for tomorrow, I see. Maybe you could play with it 100 feet above the ground."

"Hey, yeah, I could do that. It'll be a relief to leave the earth, even if it is only 100 feet above it. Maybe I can get a different perspective on my problem up there, too."

Jay's connection with the agent's murder was understandably the talk of the station. The local news media covered the murder of the agent and Jay's suspicious involvement. The other news organizations, because Jay was with a competing network, could have been ruthless, but they weren't. Judging from the coverage of the story after Jay's release it was apparent the other stations did not know who or what the agent was following. After Jay revealed to his station manager what Bob Gregg had just told him, the man's eyes lit up.

"Jay, we want you to know that you have our support in this matter. We know you were on the job at the time the agent was shot, and we know the connection is coincidence. If you need us for anything, just let us know."

"Thanks, I appreciate that." Turning to leave Jay's office, the manager had an afterthought. He paused before going through the door. "Dawson, I smell a scoop. Get the story."

Jay smiled. Could this be his big break?

He phoned the police to tell them he was going to leave town for western Virginia to repair an antenna, then he phoned Bob Gregg for an interview.

20

Jay made it to the antenna site on one of the mountains overlooking the beautiful Shenandoah National Park. He enjoyed the climb to the top of the tower leaving all the noise far below. A hundred some feet above the earth, he didn't feel bound to the problems in his life.

"If only it were true," he thought. "If only it were true. Well, can't stay up here forever. Sooner or later going to have to meet those problems head on." Securing his safety umbilical to the side of the metal structure, Jay took in the view. It was grand.

The sight of hot air balloons floating over the country side made him feel that no one had to be tied down with life's external pressures if you could just let go. Balloons were a common enough sight in town. An outrigger in one of the northern counties could arrange a flight for you if you had the fare. It was the sight of the hang gliders that really startled him. He watched the hang gliders a few moments.

"That's kind of neat," he thought. "I'd like to try that someday." He began getting lost in the experience vicariously.

"Hey, Dawson," the voice on his radio headset brought him back to the task at hand. "Never see hot air balloons before?"

Jay responded, "There's hand gliders out there, three of them. It's really a neat sight."

"Ahh, come on, I'm starving. I want to get something to eat. Forget the gliders, and get the job done. I don't want to be here all day."

"Go ahead without me if you're so hungry."

"Don't tempt me. You know the rules. No one is allowed on an antenna without a buddy below...just in case."

"Okay, okay, but I want to try my radar out on the stuff that's floating around up here."

"Just get on with it, Dawson!"

The maintenance on the antenna was routine, during which his mind flitted to different subjects: Amanda, terrorists, hang gliding, Amanda. "Amanda," he thought. "Talk about poor choice in women: a motorcycle mama. A motorcycle mama terrorist. A tattooed motorcycle mama terrorist. Definitely not someone you want to take home to Mom and Dad."

Completing his job, Jay pulled out his pocket radar device. "Son-of-a-gun! It works!" he exclaimed as he picked up one of the hot air balloons. There were three colorful balloons, and he saw each one on his radar. Shifting slightly, he panned in on the hang gliders. "Ah, shit, always a glitch," he pouted. "Back to the drawing board." He pocketed the gadget and descended the metal tower.

Jay jumped the last couple feet to the ground. When he landed, he put his hands on his hips and faced in the direction of the hang gliders. Noting Jay's perplexed look, his backup asked, "Everything check out up there?"

"The antenna's fine. It's this radar I don't understand. It registered the three hot air balloons. When I tried for the hang gliders, it only picked up two out of the three. Too bad I can't make my ex-wife disappear like that." He sighed, "I'm afraid my toy has a glitch."

"Glitch?"

"Yeah, you know, two plus one is three, but I only get two."

"Dawson, maybe you don't have a glitch," the assistant said laughing. "Maybe the answer is 21."

"It's a good thing you drove yourself, smartass. I'd have left you here starving," Jay said good naturedly. "See you back at the station tomorrow. I've got an appointment with someone in DC."

21

Arriving at Gregg's office, Jay noted it took a little longer than the usual two hours. He had forgotten how bad the traffic was in DC. Bob Gregg's secretary told Jay that Bob was on the phone and would be right with him. The two made polite conversation while Jay absently paged through a magazine, thinking over how he would approach the story. When the light on the receptionist's consul went out, indicating Bob was off the phone, the secretary let Jay into Bob's office.

"Damn, boy, it's good to see you," Gregg roared as he stepped around his desk with hand extended.

"I'm just glad to be seen anywhere but in jail," Jay answered light heartedly.

"I almost fell out of my chair when that memo came across my desk connecting you with the murder of that agent," said Gregg.

"It came as a bit of shock to me, too," Jay replied. "Fortunately, from what you're saying, the police seem to know that I'm not their man, and that's why I'm here. I need to find out more of what's happening."

"Are you asking as an interested bystander or as a reporter?" Gregg asked.

"Well, kind of both, except I'm more than just a bystander. I took it personally, you know, but the reporter in me tells me this may be a major league story."

A curtain of confidentiality and propriety came down Bob Gregg's face. "Have a seat," he said quietly. Then he walked back to his chair behind the expansive desk. Gregg sat down with a heavy sigh, then turned his chair to see the view out his window. Jay pulled up a guest chair, sat down and waited for Gregg to get comfortable. There was a respectful silence between them.

Rubbing his chin, Gregg finally said, "I can't say a damn thing to a reporter, Jay, aside from what you read in the papers. Beneath that, they have the cap so tight on this incident I can't tell you everything that is happening. The flow of information is so controlled that if anything hit the papers it wouldn't take long to figure out who leaked the information."

"I understand confidentiality, but I was arrested because of this bitch. I had to endure a night in a grungy old jail. This whole thing has not made me a happy camper. I need to know what's happening."

"Look, I know you're upset. You were in a tight spot but you're okay now."

"The hell I'm okay," Jay exploded. "I told you earlier this is getting personal."

The big chair turned around. The man sitting in it looked at Jay and said very calmly and definitively, "I am going to change the subject."

Jay knew that the man speaking was on the brink of committing an indiscretion, and that man was not yet ready to do so. Jay backed off. The timing wasn't right.

"Jay, did you know that a couple nights ago the Washington Monument had a black sack shrouding its apex? How in the hell it got there is a mystery to me. You know what the monuments in this town mean to me don't you? Well, I took that personally. I take all debasement and defilement personally. Everyone has abandoned this mystery but me, because, like you, I have taken it personally. In your case, the mystery has not been abandoned. Let the big guys figure it out."

Jay calmed down. Then something Bob Gregg said piqued his curiosity. "What's so mysterious about a monument getting shrouded? It's just the wind or another vandal who didn't care a wit about the documentary we made about America's classical architecture."

"This isn't ordinary, Jay. What makes it so mysterious is that it took place 500 feet above the ground. We've got something that has hit the Washington Monument from the top. That must have been some carrier pigeon to make that sizable a deposit. I thought about the sack being dropped from an aeroplane, but air traffic control shows nothing flying in or out of the air free zone that night."

"A mad mountain climber?"

"Would have been seen by the rangers."

"I know disrespect for property is your pet peeve. How the Washington Monument got sacked is a mind boggle. One of my pet projects is boggling, as well."

"How so?" encouraged Gregg.

"You know I'm pretty good at gadgets. Well, I don't know that this will ever have any use, but I made this really neat pocket radar device. When I was up on an antenna yesterday, I tried it out on some hot air balloons and hang gliders. The balloons all showed up, but the puzzling thing is that when I switched over to the hang gliders, two out of the three were detected. For some odd reason, my radar fouled up and couldn't pickup the third. So you see I've got a couple mysteries to work with. I'll let one go temporarily, but only temporarily."

"Thanks, Jay, I appreciate your understanding." Bob Gregg rose from his chair and came around his desk to usher Jay Dawson out. "I'm sorry your trip here didn't render more information. Don't be such a stranger," Bob told Jay again, as he extended his hand. Jay shook it.

"You know I won't be," said Jay emphatically and looked Bob Gregg straight in the eye.

Jay knew he would be coming back for the information he needed. Bob Gregg knew it, too.

22

Earlier that day, the Isuzu took the two, Eric Killian and Susan Safran, down the fire trail.

"This is Loft Mountain. It's the most accessible launch site," commented Ranger Sue. "You won't have to carry your gear but a few yards."

"This isn't very secluded," said Killian noticing the other two vehicles parked off the trail.

"I didn't want you to become discouraged on the first day having to hike too far. It's very popular with the local hang gliding club. I see them out here often, so I know it should be good flying. Maybe that's who belongs to those parked trucks."

Ranger Sue walked toward the launch site to find out what she could see. Killian was not happy. He had apparatus on this hang glider he didn't want anyone asking him about. It was a fourth generation glider, and he knew most would be curious about it.

Ranger Sue returned. "Yup, I was right. We have two other hang gliders to keep you company, and a bonus."

"Bonus?"

"Seems some hot air balloons have decided to float in this area. They're well out of the way, but they sure are a pretty sight."

"They better stay out far enough not to interfere. Do you know very much about the sport?" asked Killian innocently.

"No, nothing at all. Why do you ask?"

As Killian slipped some device from the A-frame back into the stuff sack, he continued. "I thought you might get bored watching with nothing to do."

"I won't get bored."

"All right. It's your day off."

"You're absolutely correct, Mr. Killian, and I can choose to spend it the way I wish," her hands were on her hips at this point.

"Suit yourself. No arguments here. Excuse me while I go study the slope."

"Why do you do that?"

"First of all you never explore new hills without first getting advice from someone who has flown it before. I did that before I came when I contacted the local association."

"Everyone does seem to launch from here," recalled the ranger.

"That's because the air here behaves very well. It's a bald, so the air comes up the slope very smoothly. If there were a sharp-edged cliff, some fierce turbulence could be produced as well as some areas of dead air and reverse winds."

"I guess that could be important in keeping your hang glider stable, right?"

"You catch on rather quickly, Ms. Safran. You might make a hang glider pilot yet."

"God forbid," Killian thought.

"Will all the other launch sites be okay to try?" asked Safran.

"They have all been tried," Killian responded. "The association in this park keeps good records. The six areas I've chosen, are all navigable."

"Good. Your trip here won't have been for nothing," she gave him as sweet a smile as she could.

"Shit," thought Killian reading her smile. "She has something seductive planned." Killian wanted to get aloft as soon as possible. Ranger Sue's company was beginning to try his patience. Hastily, without missing any of the finer points, he assembled his craft. Before further conversation could be initiated, he took the necessary three steps to get himself airborne.

His main purpose today was to accustom himself to how the hang glider performed. It was a new design, a new generation of hang glider. In addition he had to become familiar with all the instruments that would help him maximize his use of the air currents.

The test flight by the Washington Monument was a sample of how the equipment operated. In the mountains, two hours of testing would be enough to understand all the mechanics.

The previous test targeted the Washington Monument for three reasons. One, they wanted to see if the radar on top of the Executive Building would detect them. Radar and ordnance had been increased in the nation's capital after the Cessna had crashed just below the First Family's residence in 1994. The official word was a suicide attempt. Word in the terrorist camps was much different. Two, they wanted to see how the air currents from the Potomac River would influence the flight and operation of the hang glider. Three, if they were caught, they could explain it as a harmless prank: Eric always wanted to hang glide down the Mall in DC. Night was chosen for the prank to arouse as little concern as possible.

Naturally, due to the sensitive location of the test flight, the hang glider could not be equipped with a warhead. As a substitute for the missiles, weight was added to the A-frame by way of a sports bag filled with damp sand.

All went well with the release from the glider plane, but there was some wind sheer that climbed the monument and rendered the hang glider momentarily useless. To regain control, Eric had to jettison the sandbag. As luck would have it, the sand filled sportsbag landed on top of the monument, on the very apex of the structure. If he had tried to get the bag to land there, he probably couldn't have done it.

After a couple hours of test flying, he was ready to call it a day. At the bottom of the hill was a valley that was served by a winding road which followed a creek bed. Due to the lack of rain, only a trickle was apparent in the creek. Ranger Sue had arranged with Killian to meet him down in the valley.

Susan Safran was impressed by the sportsman. She would never have guessed that this apparently delicate looking man could have so much stamina to last two hours in flight. She could see that he had tremendous reflexes and strength. She could also see that he was also able to relax, and that was how he could pace himself to outlast even those pilots who started after him.

Killian scheduled his landing just as someone drove off and someone else came to launch. This way he didn't have to answer any questions. He knew the black hang glider was drawing stares from the other pilots. Rehydrating himself, he decided not to launch from a different point. "Let's save the other launches for tomorrow," he suggested.

"I'm glad you decided that," said Ranger Sue. "You are cordially invited to dinner at my cabin this evening," and she struck out walking toward the thin stream.

"Hey, where are you going?" shouted Killian, puzzled.

"I know a short cut. Besides I've been meaning to check on the shored up banks of this stream, farther on down. See you at six," she waved and disappeared behind some trees.

Killian couldn't believe it. He wanted to get rid of her, didn't know how, and there she went without him having to say anything. He wanted her to return so he could make her go away on his authority, not hers.

Getting into the four by four, he started the winding journey back to his camp.

23

After driving back to camp, Killian took a shower before walking over to Ranger Sue's cabin for dinner. As he walked he thought, "Sleeping in a regular bed might not be such a bad idea. A bit of seductive sport might be just what the doctor ordered."

As he approached the cabin, he noticed hers was one of five in a compound but more secluded than the rest. It was painted a wonderful shade of brown, "A shade of brown only the Park Service is able to purchase," thought Killian. "A bear would have to think twice before moving in."

Ranger Sue met him as he walked up the three steps to her front porch. "Hey, Irish. Welcome to Mudsop Stop."

"What's that?"

"It's a name dedicated to the shade of brown these cabins have been doused with."

"Yes, I couldn't help but notice that wonderful color. Is Mr. Mudsop dead and buried?"

"That's funny. Come on in." She turned and entered the cabin.

Killian then got a little nervous. He was concerned about the possibility of discovery. He knew park rangers were not as paranoid as regular police, but they could still be as dangerous. Eric Killian did not see how he could relax just yet.

Ranger Sue realized that Killian had not followed her in through the front door. She returned to his side where he was surveying the camp on the front porch. Misreading him she said, "This is my favorite time of day and my favorite spot. This cabin, although not much to look at, has the best view of all the cabins. Sometimes I just like to sit out here at night and drink in the view. I can tell you enjoy it also, Eric."

The sound of his name and her hand on his arm pulled Killian from his train of thought. "Sorry," he offered, "I got lost in the scenery and didn't hear you."

"Great view, huh?"

"Yeah, just great."

"By the way, I won't be able to watch you hang glide tomorrow."

"Oh?"

"I'm filling in at another station for someone who's taking the day off."

"Well then, we'd better make the most of this evening," said Killian turning toward the door. He slipped his hand under the ranger's elbow. "Now, where is that great American dinner you were going to fix me?"

Dinner was set at the table as they walked through the front door. Ranger Sue had outdone herself with a cold primavera salad, crusty bread and a couple of smuggled bottles of Chianti. All through dinner, as the wine bottles emptied, Ranger Safran leaned in closer and closer to Killian.

He knew with her body language what was coming. Safran knew how to send the right signals. Red wine proved to be the right elixir. He knew he was about to discover whether there was anything attractive beneath her ugly park-issued clothing.

With all this knowledge going on, Killian found himself at the mercy of her drunkenness. She fell on top of him at the table.

"Wouldn't we be more comfortable in your bed?" he asked.

"I rather liked this position, myself," she said laughing. Safran slid to the floor between his legs. She slid her arms along his thighs and traced the inseam of his jeans with the palms of her hands.

"You're rather slow and deliberate with those hands, aren't you?" smiled Killian.

"The better to feel you with, my dear," she giggled.

"I do believe you are drunk, my pet ranger."

"Loose, Mr. Killian, real loose." She tossed her head and began to unfasten his belt.

Killian leaned back and let her have her way with him. He was beginning to relax and enjoy himself.

24

After a twenty-four hour search, Bob Gregg was absolutely baffled. Combing the area for anything unusual, the squad had found nothing, not even a catapult. Everything appeared normal, although nothing felt normal. There was no logical explanation for how the cargo sack became affixed to the top of the Washington Monument.

It was like Dawson's radar. Two and one didn't add up to three. It kept looking more and more like twenty-one.

Gregg was near the monument, so he decided to walk over to it. Maybe an ant could tell him what went on. It was the middle of the day and the air was cold and so was the ground. At least it was hard. Bob Gregg decided to lie on it anyway, despite his designer appearance. He wanted to see the monument from the ground up. "If you want an ant's perspective, maybe you need to become an ant," he thought.

Gregg couldn't help but notice some of the odd looks he was getting from passersby. He didn't care. He needed a new slant on the situation.

"It's been ages since I've been caught lying down on the job," he continued to talk to himself. "Two and one become twenty-one when you don't add, but you join. Boy, how dippy can you get! Well, let's see, what can we join? What other weird things have been going on? What's relative, or is that relevant?"

Bob Gregg began to lose his train of thought. First it was on what his wife was fixing for dinner that night, then what was good on television. The third in the series of that mystery program would ire this evening. "That old TV lawyer could probably figure this one out in a heartbeat. I wonder how he would go about it."

Then his mind began to wander as he thought of the fishing he'd do when he retired. "Maybe I'll do something strange, like sky diving or parasailing. Wonder if I could do hang gliding. With my luck I'd get killed first time out. Killed, maybe not with a gun like that agent, but killed. Then I could hang glide with the angels. No one would see me then, kind of a stealth angel," he chuckled to himself. "Spirits don't need radar, they are radar," and he stopped short. "Oh, my God! That's what Jay saw or didn't see," he said aloud and jumped from the ground and ran back to his car. "God, that's it," and he sped to his office. He phoned ahead to have his secretary reach Jay Dawson. "Tell him to drop everything and get to D.C. as soon as possible," he directed his secretary.

Jay was in his office when Gregg's secretary phoned. "What does he want?" Jay asked.

"I don't know. He phoned from his car. He sounded excited, so I'd say the sooner you got here the better."

"Thanks. I'm on my way." Jay wondered if Gregg finally came to his senses about disclosing the information about the terrorists.

Jay Dawson was admitted to Bob Gregg's office without formality. Bob Gregg was standing with his back to the door, looking out his windows. Jay entered, closed the door quietly, and sat down without greeting. He knew Bob Gregg would talk when he was ready.

"There is an informant within the CCPU, that is the Command Council for Protestant Ulster. The State Department and FBI have received information of an impending terrorist attack aimed at the United States. There are several aspects of this news which lend it a fair amount of credence.

"First, a team of terrorists was developed which combined the brightest and most effective individuals available.

"Second, each team member entered the United States under various guises and each utilized a separate port of entry. Two of the names provided by the CCPU have been checked through immigration. The other names are not known, but we have reason to believe the Blackhawk is organizing them.

"Amanda Shahey matches one of the descriptions. We believe she may be anywhere from Florida to DC. The other, Eric Michaels, whom we believe is traveling on a passport under Eric Killian, entered through Seattle, Washington a few weeks ago. His present whereabouts are not known. Although my guess would be that he is near Shahey.

"Third, intelligence has pieced together a plot to orchestrate a terrorist attack within the United States. Various terrorist groups, Italy's Red Brigade, Germany's Beider Manhoff Gan and even Lebanon's Ayotollah have all planned actions on US soil. All but the actions on the New York trade center in 1993 and the spectacular collapse of the Seattle Space Needle in 1995 have been thwarted. The CCPU nurtures and receives a level of support in the United

States. This provides them with a network in the event of any action.

"The FBI started surveillance on known CCPU supporters immediately after it was confirmed two of the terrorist team had entered the country. Auditing of bank accounts shows increased activity in accounts of several of the supporters. The clincher came yesterday when the pieces of the body of a daughter of one of the supporters was found in a car that had been blown to bits at a bar outside Quantico. The worst part is she was a sergeant in the Marine Corp. It may be coincidence, but they are checking everything.

"British intelligence was working with us on tracking down this team. The agent that was killed was closing in on Amanda. He had reported to his colleagues that he intended to arrest her the day he was shot. Unfortunately, it didn't work out the way he planned.

"There is a fair amount of guesswork going on by the experts, but they feel an attack is imminent. Given the death of the Sergeant, most are guessing it will be in DC. The target is still an unknown."

Here, Bob Gregg turned around to face his desk. It was the first time through his dissertation that he acknowledged Jay being there. "Oh, Dawson, I didn't hear you come in. Glad you're here though, I wanted to speak to you about your radar problem."

Jay could see through the ruse, and played along. "Oh yeah, hi. I was off in a world of my own. Sorry, I wasn't listening, was any of what you said for me?"

"No, son," said Gregg smiling. "I was just talking to myself. Now about those hang gliders, particularly the one that didn't register on the radar. What's the possibility that one could be stealth?"

25

The test for firing the missile went remarkably well. Killian chose a slope with a slight incline so that he could climb the hill without much difficulty.

Firing the missile was easy. It was adjusting his weight to compensate for the back thrust that he had to master. After three tries, he could hit his target dead center. Three more successful attempts and he was on his way to his last and final launch site.

Despite the enjoyment Killian received from this sport, he was tense. The moment of his objective was at hand. All had to be right to succeed, and weather provided the biggest set of variables, but having studied the patterns for the last few years, he knew that the DC area was entering a stable period.

Autumn was like that in most parts of the world. That is, you could depend on predictable conditions. The mornings and evenings would be cool with the afternoons very warm.

The warm afternoons would heat the cities and countrysides to create warm air rising and sustain a flight. Cool air would make you go faster in a straight line for a longer length of time.

He wished he could make this a solitary act, but he needed a launch and a pickup. Maybe he could convince Chessie that Amanda's help was unnecessary.

The Isuzu came to a crunching halt on the fire road. Engulfed by its dust trail, the machine resembled a shadow of itself. An inestimable amount of red dust camouflaged the original green paint well against the autumn backdrop of the Blue Ridge Mountains. This suited Eric Killian's future purpose of deceit handsomely.

Turning off the Isuzu's engine, Killian descended and unstrapped the dust covered case on the roof. Pulling it to the ground, he then removed a twenty-foot-long black zip bag. Sliding the contents from the rip stop material, he allowed the fabric to unfurl.

At this point of assemblage, he always thought of a giant moth emerging from it crysalis. With the aid of a matte finished black superstructure, the would-be insect took on the look of a hang glider-----a very expensive and very well kept hang glider.

This was a customized hang glider made of carbon fiber. It had a double surface and was very stable.

The fire road ended right where Killian had stopped. A few yards ahead there was a bald overlook. From the overlook there was a grand view of the Shenandoah Valley.

There was no such thing as a bad view. Each new launch point presented a different aspect of this valley, and Killian was continuously amazed.

Eric Killian had seen beautiful spots in his native Ireland and even in Great Britain, but there was vastness in the United States that could not fit into a country the size of the United Kingdom, and its island neighbors.

The geographical features are constant for miles in the US. so the thermals are unbelievably reliable. Eric loved flying in the States. No matter how bad the conditions, he had flown in worse in Great Britain.

Because he learned to use the elements so efficiently in his country, in the optimum conditions in the States Eric was top notch. He had flown in weather most others countries wouldn't even get out of bed for.

As an accomplished sportsman, with a pilot 3 license, he had done some cross country soaring in England from Bristol to Bournemouth. Eric had several trophies to his name for the competitions he had entered.

What had attracted him to the sport was its independence. He could carry his aircraft up any hill and fly without the need of a motor.

This bald was perfect for launching the hang glider. The shape of the slope was gradual and well rounded at the top. Because the top was bald, that is an absence of trees, shrubs and grasses, it made an excellent site for landing.

Eric had gotten the difficulty ratings for these from the local flying clubs. Of course weather always altered those ratings, so one had to be a meteorologist of sorts.

On a day like this which was windless, this slope had a rating of five. On a scale of one to ten, it was of medium difficulty. If there was a wind of five knots, it would have been a seven.

The bald was unpopular with hikers and picnickers, due to its uneasy access, but even so, at this time of the year, and this day of the week, no one was around.

Nearly assembled, the hang glider took on pterodactyl proportions.   Any fool can hang glide, he had been advised, but not for long. Eric Killian was no fool. He was a

professional in more than one aspect of life. He had the
awards and the bank account to prove it.

One of the greatest lessons hang gliding had taught the
man was tempering his enthusiasm with patience. He knew
of more than one operation meeting with failure because of
untempered personalities. None of these failures was his.

It was a stern discipline, but he had persevered and had
become expert. Now it was his way of escaping.

He had taken up the sport because he had always
wanted to get away where no one could bother him. At the
same time he wanted to be able to use his own cunning to
survive.

His career as a mercenary helped to subsidize his habit,
and this sport gave a different slant to some of his
assignments. Often he could think through an operation by
getting aloft. Given the aspect of height, you get a greater
picture, which aids in your three dimensional way of thinking.

Having completed his primary objective, he was going
to have fun. He packed up and went to a more accessible
sight.

During the assembly, Killian heard the grind of a
Jeep's transmission echo through the valley. He also detected
twigs snapping behind him. It was probably Ranger Sue
making sure she didn't miss anything.

He strapped himself into the glider and hoisted the rig
up and walked over to the edge of the bald. As he waited for
the right moment for takeoff he heard the ranger's familiar
voice.

"Where's your hurry, Mr. Eric?" came her drawl
tainted with sensuality.

Ignoring her, he took two strides into the wind and
was airborne.

Safran had become a nuisance. She was getting in the
way. Jumping off the bald was his way of ignoring her. Eric
couldn't have been more satisfied if he had smacked her

across the face. Ranger Sue, had been a tremendous help in finding the good launch sites. He exploited her for her expertise, but despised her at the same time.

She considered herself the last of the great frontier women as well as God's oversexed gift to man. When she wasn't spouting ceaseless wilderness commentary, she was providing a continuous sexual taunt.

It was good to have a park ranger accompany you through otherwise inaccessible parts of the national forest, but he was tired of the fact she only had two modes of oral delivery, three if you considered her silent performance in bed.

Her usefulness had just about run out and Eric looked forward to retiring her from the Park Service in a permanent way. It also meant one less person to connect him with anything unusual happening in the area.

Once airborne, he was relieved to be suspended in flight. The rush of the wind excited his senses, and he relaxed into the concentration needed to navigate the conditions properly.

He swung his body so he would turn easily along the ridge. Slowly the great bird rose as the wind steadied into an updraft. Killian estimated he was fifty feet above the ridge. There was a continuous, unconscious adjustment as his body balanced against the little gusts and surges of air, as he tried to keep within the narrow band of the lift. An extra surge of lift hit him as the thermal flowed up the warm sunny face of the hill. He took it with his muscles and turned and slowed to maximize the bonus.

Chasing a sparrow along the ridge, he tried to gain altitude by the cunning use of the elusive surges. After a half hour he began to plan his descent. Finally he landed touching lightly and expertly on the bald hill top, where he began his flight.

Eric always wore leather when hang gliding. It offered more protection and warmth than any other material. The man had low blood pressure and was often cold in hot weather. This body induced coolness seldom gave rise to impatience or loss of temper. Because he was good at suppressing his anger he sailed on even keel most of the time. His anger was released in his mercenary tactics. Eric took pride in this. It was a specific trait of his to be able to keep calm in the middle of chaos. To this he attributed his rate of success.

The fundamental rule of learning to hang glide is to try only one new thing at a time. Never tackle another variable until you've got the one thing right. Eric applied this to his work as a mercenary, and it was how he had gotten his reputation.

He started out slow and simple. After he mastered the simpler type of operation, he took on bigger ones. His confidence level was high but he still knew what his limitations were, and he weighed these limitations with each new job and risk he took.

When his limitations put him too much at risk, he called in help. It was then and only then that he didn't work alone. To his way of thinking, taking the solitary approach was the only way to guarantee any measure of success.

He laughed when he thought of flying. In itself, it is not dangerous. It is the landing and the taking off that are. Aviation is terribly unforgiving of any carelessness, incapacity or neglect. This theorem, too, he incorporated into his operations.

Any hang gliding association will advise against flying alone. Having a spectator was good, if only it wasn't this woman. No hang gliding association could possibly imagine what he had been up to that morning.

When Eric had landed, Susan was still there. She came to greet him. As usual she was in uniform. Because the temperatures were still quite warm, she was wearing shorts. Wherever she was and whatever she wore, she always walked in those same ugly rock climbing boots.

As he watched her sway in his direction, he thought she gave a sexy meaning to the word ugly. Although he didn't particularly care for the woman, it would be a shame to have to waste that lovely body.

Susan Safran couldn't take her eyes off Eric as he expertly landed the black wedge. She saw his muscles bulge beneath his shirt. Exhilaration swept through her body as she watched him seductively glide against the blue sky. Her veins were mainlining excitement as she slowly approached him.

Eric focused on disassembling the hang glider and didn't acknowledge the ranger standing close to him. She fingered the craft's black matte finish, and then straddled the kingpost.

"What's your hurry?" Susan Safran asked quietly moving the post up and down her leg. Killian took the post from her and slid it into the sack, then silently shouldered the pack and walked purposefully around to the back of the Isuzu.

"I said, what's your hurry?" Ranger Sue slowly followed in his steps. At the back of the Trooper, she began swinging playfully on its back door. When that didn't get his attention, she detached herself from the door and let her arm extend to Eric's shoulder. As that hand caressed his arm and began tracing his belt line to the buckle, she was rubbing her ample breasts against the sleeve of his leather jacket. "This is a very secluded spot and you seem so uptight. I think you could use a little tension relief. What do you say, Irish?" she said in huskier tones.

Eric pushed her away and began sliding the black nylon fabric on top of the vehicle. "I hate being called that, bitch. Don't say it again," he said cruelly through clenched teeth.

Uncertain of his meaning but attracted by this display of brutal emotion, Ranger Sue smiled as she began unbuttoning her shirt. Killian slowly turned from the back of the vehicle. As her breasts became exposed, he thought again what a waste, but he grabbed her by the arms and pulled her in close to his chest.

Safran got even more pumped up thinking that this was really going to be good. She closed her eyes waiting for his next move. Killian moved his hands from her arms to her throat and at the last minute repressed the urge to kill her. He could have put an end to her lurid anticipation in one martial art second, but he thought twice.

He had to admit she had been a genius for getting them to remote and secluded areas. Besides, he wasn't getting paid for this action. Instead of killing her, he threw her to the ground. He was not going to jeopardize the mission by killing her.

"Not here, bitch," he spat. "Get to your cabin." Then as an afterthought, he smiled.

*   *   *

Back at her cabin, Susan Safran felt a rush from the day's hang glider watching. As a result she was thoroughly turned on by the sight of Eric Killian. His intensity had continued when they returned to her cabin.

He had shoved her into the bedroom and would have ripped her clothes off if she had not done so first.

Ranger Sue had the misconception that the redheaded man knew exactly how to please her because of his ability to get her to orgasm. His love making was fierce, almost violent, but she loved every moment of it. He did it only to please himself. She was totally sated. Where had he learned to use his tongue like that? He was an expert in more than one field. She could see that, and she wasn't about to let him get away.   Not without having more sex.   Her first impressions of him as being strange and soppy were forever obscured by a stronger image of his forcefulness and intensity.

26

"Stealth?" repeated Jay, questioning the possibility. "That would certainly explain it. The device checked out when I got it home, so that could be the only explanation other than it was an hallucination."

"What if that canvas bag on the Washington Monument has something to do with a hang glider?"

"Anything is possible, but where's it going to launch from?"

"That's where I get stuck, too," Bob Gregg said dejectedly.

There was a pause in the conversation. Then Jay picked it up again. "You know, even if that is what's happening, it's not much to go on."

"My intuition isn't much to go on either, but I have a hunch the attack is going to be close. Well, that's all I wanted to mention. Stealth, I mean. So, thanks for coming."

"Yeah, sure," Jay said feeling a bit dismissed. "Keep in touch," he added as he left Bob Gregg grumbling over his daily mail.

The door to Gregg's office had closed when he finished reading a memo. He looked up with a start, then ran out. "Dawson. Which way did he go?" he shouted at his secretary, as he ran from the office.

"To the elevators, I would guess, Sir."

Halfway to the elevator he spotted Jay. He squelched the desire to shout for him. Instead he walked quickly and grabbed him by the shoulder and spun him around.

"What the...," exclaimed Jay at the suddenness of the about face.

Gregg nervously looked up and down the hallway before handing Jay the paper. "Look at this," he half whispered.

The memo, written by Antiterrorist Intelligence (ATI), was an update on the missing terrorists. The government's informant indicated one member of the terrorist group to be Eric Michaels.

ATI had attached a biography of Michaels to the memo, complete with picture. "Boy, talk about fitting the psychological profile of a terrorist," Jay said walking with Gregg to his office. "Loner, former military pilot, dishonorably discharged for insubordination...hey, now here's something interesting. This guy is a world class hang glider expert."

Jay Dawson looked up from the memo into Bob Gregg's face.

"Bingo," they said in unison.

Once again sitting across from Bob Gregg, the investigative mind of Jay Dawson began to work.

"Okay, what have we got here? A group of terrorists, two identities known; a bankroll; a dead Marine Sergeant; an unsolved vandalism; a stealth hang glider; a rumor of a terrorist attack; an unknown target within Washington, DC----"

"We don't know it's DC," interrupted Gregg.

"I say it is. Where else in the US can terrorists make a greater impact, unless the President is else where in the nation?"

"Who says it's the President?"

"I do. I have intuition, too, you know. Beside that, why else would they be in DC?"

"If you recall," Bob Gregg said, "I was not the one to say they were."

"Ever the devil's advocate," soothed Jay. Then getting excited he began again. "Bob, let's complete this one scenario. After it's complete, then let's see where the holes are."

"You're right. Let's Blue Sky the blasted thing," said Bob Gregg getting into the spirit of it.

Jay got up from his chair and began pacing Gregg's office. At first he rubbed his chin, and uttered a hmm every now and again. Then he began pointing while he walked and talked. "Where would you go if you wanted to hang glide? There is a concession in Nags Head, North Carolina where they teach you to glide over the sand dunes. But this guy is an expert. He would be far beyond Sand Dunes."

"Why not the Eastern Shore?"

"Possibly. There are some outcroppings on the shore of the Chesapeake Bay, but they are pretty much secluded. Where would you stay?"

"See what you mean. How about the Shenandoah Valley, Appalachian Mountains. There would be plenty of hotels or camp grounds where you wouldn't arouse much scrutiny," Bob Gregg offered.

"How much you want to bet Killian was flying the stealth up by the Blue Ridge, where I saw those hang gliders?"

"It just takes one phone call to get the park registers. Let's see what that turns up.   You just might be onto something, boy," offered Bob Gregg, returning to his Southern mode. Jay smiled. When Gregg got to talking like that, he knew he was firing with all his cylinders.

27

Amanda Shahey thought she had eliminated all the obstacles in the way of her rendezvous with Eric Killian. There was that agent in Florida who recognized her deplaning from Rio. Then the other agent who tailed her to North Carolina. She laughed. In the bar, without knowing who she was, he had been hot after her tail. She threw the FBI off her scent by framing Jay Dawson. Too bad. Dawson really was genuinely decent and good. But, she thought, all's fair in love and terrorism.

Arriving at the designated campground on Skyline Drive, Shahey checked the registration sheet for Killian.

"Who you looking for, Miss?" asked the ranger on duty.

"Killian. Eric Killian."

"He's at sight seven, but you won't find him there. I saw him drive off with Ranger Sue. Probably at her cabin. Can I give you directions?"

Shahey was not surprised. "Don't bother!" she retorted and turning on her heel, stomped out the door.

In front of Killian's tent, she knew there was yet another obstacle to be removed, this Ranger Sue character. "Up to his old unoriginal tricks," she thought spying a wine bottle tucked inside the camping gear. "The same ploy to get whomever it was into bed with him."

She looked around her and saw no humans. Taking off her helmet, she balanced her Harley and got off the bike.

It was nearly seven o'clock and the trip up to Skyline Drive had made Amanda tired. She decided to take advantage of the tent and crawled into it and fell asleep for the night.

* * *

Killian rose at dawn and dressed without rousing Ranger Sue from her sleep. The previous night had relieved a lot of tension, but he didn't want Safran to accompany him on his flying expeditions today.

Killian returned to his camp sight to get some coffee before heading out toward another launch site. Amanda had awakened early as well and was sitting on a log at the fire ring.

"You're early, Shahey," he greeted critically.

"Can't cope with a little riffle in the plans, Red?"

"I can cope with anything but incompetence from team members. You call yourself a professional? You're nothing but a fuckup, Shahey. What the hell were you thinking killing those two agents?"

"What would you have suggested? They were on to me."

"How?"

"They were sipping Pina Coladas in customs when I came through. How the hell should I know? He was there.

He recognized me from Libya. Had to kill him. As for the one in South Carolina, he was good enough to make the find but not good enough to make the catch. What else you want to know?"

"One of these days your luck is going to run out. Just make sure your judgement doesn't get clouded."

"You should talk, asshole. How do you expect to keep a clear head with red wine and American pie? Thinking with your dick again?"

"Nope," he said easing his way to the ground. "Feeling my way slowly and deliberately. Would you like to get slow and deliberate, Amanda, my dear?"

"That's not why we're here. Keep it straight in your mind, not in some bitches pants."

"Jealous are we now, Darlin'? Getting a bit ruffled?"

Amanda ignored his taunts. "What have you got to eat around here?" she asked kicking the cooler.

"Take whatever you can find. I'm leaving. See you later if you're still here." He got into his Trooper and left Amanda standing at his tent scowling.

Before entering the highway, Killian looked at his maps. Getting his bearings, he turned right toward his first take off point for the day. Today would be just for fun.

As he drove north, he enjoyed the countryside. He thought to himself, "This really is pretty. Too bad I can't enjoy it more. Maybe when I'm old and retired I'll return. Hah, now there's a joke. Consider this, a retired terrorist. I wonder what kind of pension I'll collect. In a week I could be dead unless this mission goes without a hitch."

Killian slowed as he passed the sign indicating Mid Ridge Bulge Parking Area. Taking the next left, he parked the Trooper and jumped out. He took a few deep breaths of fresh air. Dew was still on the waist high grass. It was parted only by a foot path receding into the trees. "What a glorious day to fly," Killian whispered slinging the hang glider over his shoulder. He began his trek into the trees.

Having walked a mile and a quarter into the woods, Killian looked at his map to figure where he needed to get off the path. "A quarter of a mile more and I should be at the rock outcropping I'm looking for."

Back at her cabin, Susan Safran groggily reached over the bed to touch Eric Killian. She looked up to see that he had left without a trace. Laying her head back down, Ranger Sue let a look of disgust show on her face. "It's only eight o'clock and he's already gone. That has to be some kind of a record for early departures. Usually they at least stay for breakfast."

As she tried to get out of bed the red wine reminded her of how much she drank last night. "Oooh," she moaned, "I'm glad I don't have to report until later. Think I'll stay in bed a while longer."

28

Finally rising, Susan Safran showered and dressed for her evening shift. Before checking in she decided to drive around the camp ground to Killian's site.

She was not surprised by the absence of his truck but she was surprised by the sight of a Harley Davidson motorcycle and a woman sitting astride it. With her best official swagger, she approached the woman.

Amanda saw the female ranger approach her. She swung her leg over the saddle and stood with arms akimbo facing the approaching Safran.

"This camp site is registered to an Eric Killian. Is he here?" Safran asked.

"Sweetheart, he ain't here, hasn't been here, and if he shows up you had better be nearby because he is going to need your help."

"Who are you?" Ranger Sue asked not really wanting to hear the answer.

"I'm his girlfriend. And who are you, the reason he hasn't been here?"

Susan Safran felt herself blushing, so she pivoted on her toes and walked away. Amanda Shahey knew the answer without Safran uttering a word. "Well, I certainly hope you two have been enjoying yourself." Shahey decided it was time for a fire, so she turned and walked toward the tree line and entered the woods. Glancing over her shoulder, she saw the ranger was coming toward her. Shahey ignored her and walked deeper into the woods. She walked down a hill until she reached a dry wash. There she began picking up kindling for a fire.

Susan Safran was not one to be ignored, so she pursued Amanda into the woods. As she walked up to Shahey, she placed her hand on Amanda's shoulder. "Excuse me. I was talking to you," said Ranger Sue a bit perturbed.

"Oh, I'm sorry," Shahey said feebly, "I didn't hear you. How can I help you, Ranger?"

The ranger couldn't believe this insolence, but she carried on in her official tone of voice. "Has Mr. Killian returned yet? I wanted to say good-bye."

"Honey, get one thing straight. He never says good-bye."

Realizing an intelligent conversation with this woman would not be likely, Susan Safran turned and began walking back up the hill toward the camp site. Amanda seized the opportunity and took the knife that was hiding in her riding boots. With her right arm around Safran's neck, Shahey plunged the knife, to the hilt, into the ranger's left side. Only a slight whimper was exhaled before she collapsed against the motorcycle woman. Amanda let her fall to the ground.

Wiping the blade on the uniform sleeve, Amanda stared down at the dead figure. "Textbook," Amanda thought. Grabbing Susan under her arms, Amanda dragged the dead body further down to the wash. There she covered it with leaves and branches, and stepped back to admire her handy work. Taking a branch from the ground, Amanda spread leaves over the marks left by Susan's boots as she was dragged across the ground.

Assuring herself that there was no sign of a struggle, Amanda began collecting kindling again. Looking at the front of her jacket, she noticed there was a stain of blood. Apparently left when Susan fell against her. Amanda took off the jacket and used it as a sling for carrying the firewood back to camp.

When she reached the fireplace, Amanda placed the firewood bundle, jacket and all, inside. Setting a match to the dried twigs, she made certain the fire engulfed her jacket.

When Killian returned, Amanda had a good fire started and was adding more branches to the flames. "There are some groceries in the truck if you want to go get them," Killian informed Amanda. "I thought we could enjoy some hot dogs tonight." Killian crawled into his tent to put on some warmer clothes. Amanda gave his retiring body a look of disgust, then went to the truck for the groceries. When Killian climbed out of the tent, he saw Amanda grilling the franks.

"Have you enjoyed yourself today, Mr. Killian?" asked Amanda as he approached the fire.

"Enjoyed myself? I'm on a mission. I could crash each time I go out there. How can you ask such a question?" Killian pretended to be hurt, as he grabbed his heart. "Where would we be if that happened?"

"I'm sure your little ranger friend would have loved to put Humpty Dumpty back together again."

"My, my, Amanda, catty aren't we? I didn't know you cared."

"Care, my butt. You jeopardized this entire mission for a piece of all American ranger ass. How could you be so stupid? What if-----"

"What if what?" Killian began. "She finds out what we are doing here? Come on! How is she going to do that? She's a ranger not a mind reader."

"Well, Mr. Smart Ass Killian, we no longer have to worry about her poking her nose around here, or you poking her either, for that matter. She's out of the picture, eliminated by yours truly." Amanda took a bow.

Killian jumped up and came at Shahey so fast, she did not have time to think. He had her by the shirt, and three inches off the ground. "Why the hell did you do that? You stupid bitch, you stupid c..." Killian stopped. He knew he was homicidal for the second time in two days. He wasn't yelling but his face was very red. Shahey knew she had pressed too hard. He released her from his grip. "Get on your bike. We're leaving now." He pulled what he could from the tent and threw it into the back of the Isuzu. He left the tent, and the camp fire. He was hungry, so he grabbed a raw hot dog and jumped into the Isuzu. "Follow me. We're off to Chessie's."

29

Bob Gregg was sitting at his desk, sipping scotch, neat, and wondering why the hell Park Service Information hadn't yet responded to his request.

"Hell," he muttered to himself. "If after thirty-none years of service I can't pick up the phone and get information for myself I need to find a new job." Once again he phoned, impatiently, waiting for an answer at the other end.

"Park Service Information," came the disembodied voice.

"Yeah, this is Bob Gregg. "It's seven-goddam-o'clock and I phoned an hour and a half ago. Do you have the answer to my request?"

"No, Sir, we don't. Your request came to us after all the regular staff went home. Sir, your call did come in after 5:30."

"Looky here," Gregg interrupted, keeping his voice calm and low. "There's no need for a lecture. I don't care if you have to call your flipping' division head and get him there to push the buttons, but I want that information and I wanted it yesterday." Very quietly he continued. "Now---and I punctuate that word, now---fax that information to me in the next thirty minutes or you and your boss won't have to worry about reporting to work in the morning." He paused. "Now, what's my name?"

"Bob Gregg, Sir."

"For whom do I work?"

"ATI, Mr. Gregg, Sir."

"And where are you going to fax that information?"

"To your office, Sir."

"And when are you going to fax it?"

"In the next 30 minutes, sir."

"Make it twenty, and I'll treat you to dinner." Gregg hung up. What Jay had told him made too much sense to let it ride until tomorrow. If that was Killian hang gliding with a stealth, chances were very good that he was camping along Skyline Drive somewhere.

Bob had phoned the information service and told them to fax him a list of all campers registered in the Shenandoah Valley who were at the park in the last three weeks under the name of Eric or Killian or Red or Michaels. The problem would arise if he registered under a totally different name.

Twenty-eight minutes later Gregg's fax machine received the transmission from the Park Service. The report was a short one. Somebody at the service had used their head and compiled the report using the three names together. There was no one listed by the name of Red. Three listings came for individuals with the first name of Eric but there was only one Killian, a Killian, Eric J.

Gregg put down the paper, picked up his phone and called the head of ATI. He would be remiss in his duty if he failed to share this information and act on his own.

"The guesswork is over," he announced to the agent in charge. He relayed what information he knew. "I suggest we get some authority out to the campground to arrest Killian immediately before he slips away."

"I agree," came the agent's voice, and both men hung up the phone.

Gregg looked up at Jay. "We believe we found our boy out on the Skyline Drive in one of the campgrounds."

"Super! That fast?" replied Jay. "When do you plan to move?"

"In a couple hours. ATI is getting that all organized."

"Uh, Gregg, I'd move sooner. Something tells me that as quickly as you got the information, it's gonna take twice as long to get your hooks into this guy."

"Don't worry. There's a ranger and a state trooper out there keeping their eye on him, but not arresting him. ATI wants to use military personnel who are trained in terrorist activity to apprehend him."

"Keep your fingers crossed. It's been too easy to this point."

"Great! I can get the whole story from the front seat in your chopper."

"Whoa, boy. You are not getting in my chopper," Gregg stated most emphatically.

"Why not?"

"You're a civilian. There's a possibility of gunfire."

"Good point. Hold on while I get the station manager on the line." A minute later Jay told Gregg, "Use of the helicopter has been approved with the sole qualifier being a cameraman go along. Should we meet at Dulles?"

"No. We have a pad on the top of the building. Have him put it down here."

Arrangements were made. The news helicopter was on its way.

30

A Virginia State Patrol car drove up to the ranger station at the entrance to the Skyline Drive campsite. The ranger on duty came out to greet the trooper before he had a chance to get out of his car.

"I understand you are looking for this Killian character," the ranger started.

"That's right. Do you know where his campsite is?"

"Yeah, we know, but he's not there right now."

"Oh? You went looking for him?" There was no inflection in the trooper's tone.

"Didn't have to. A few minutes before your call came through, Killian drove out of here with some babe following him on a Harley." The trooper looked up at the ranger very quietly and widened his eyes as a cue for the ranger to offer more information. None came.

"And?" said the trooper beginning to show a slight touch of irritation.

"I wouldn't worry, he pretty much comes and goes all of the time. Besides he's got the itch for one of the female rangers here. She was due to sign in five minutes ago. When she does report, she may have an idea where he went."

Holding onto the steering wheel, the trooper asked another question with the same touch of irritation. "Did you check the campsite after getting the phone call from your base?"

"Well, no," replied the ranger. "He's registered until tomorrow, and like I said, he comes and goes all the time."

"Mr. Ranger, Sir," began the trooper with the slightest edge of sarcasm. "during your tenure of employment, have you ever experienced any camper checking out early?"

The young ranger swallowed hard. "He's over in site seven, by the woods. I'll come with you before it's completely dark," he said getting into the car.

In the growing darkness the patrol car pulled up to the campsite. Both men got out to inspect. Through the headlights they could see tents and a fire in the fire ring, burnt hot dogs on the grill, but no vehicles. There were sleeping bags, food containers, cooking pots. The disarray suggested it had been abandoned in a hurry.

The trooper grabbed the microphone from his radio and barked short staccato phrases on the updated situation to his headquarters. "By the way, the motorcyclist was a woman." His watch commander advised he stay on the scene until further instructions were received from D.C., and be there to meet a Huey.

"DC?" the ranger asked. "I thought you were based locally."

"I am," the trooper replied. "But this detail is taking orders from Washington. He's been gone over an hour in any direction at this point. At least we have a description of the vehicle and his license number." The men drove to the field designated by command headquarters.

A few moments later, the tell tale thump of a Huey helicopter could be heard nearing the camp ground. The trooper switched on his pursuit lights as well as his headlights to illuminate the field where the chopper was to land.

As the chopper maneuvered, the ranger and trooper climbed out of the cruiser. Both grabbed their caps before the down wash of the helicopter blew them away. When the craft finally settled, six commando-like men exited followed by one civilian.

One of the six, clearly the commander, walked toward the trooper, the civilian, Bob Gregg, accompanied him. The commander spoke first. "Thanks for your update. The descriptions and license number have been radioed to all police units in the western portion of the state. Since we don't know which way they went, all jurisdictions west of Richmond have been advised. With a little luck we'll catch them.

"Your update mentioned there was a connection between him and one of the rangers. Is she available?" Gregg asked.

"Well, uh, uh, yeah, Susan Safran. She was due to sign on a half hour ago. She should be at the registration building now."

"Fine, ranger, can we go there now?" Gregg asked irritably as the young man showed no signs of moving.

"Right, right. This way, Sir," he replied holding out his hand to show the way. He was still suffering from the helicopters arrival and the men with M-16s.

On the way to the registration building, Bob Gregg thought to himself, "I wonder if the woman on the motorcycle is Amanda Shahey."

Reaching the park office, the party found it vacant. They checked the duty roster. Safran's name was absent.

"That's unusual," the ranger said puzzled.   "Susan is never late. This is so out of character for her."

"When was the last time any one saw Susan Safran?" the army man asked.

31

Circling the campsite, Jay, his cameraman and pilot waited for permission to land in the open field. Even now, Gregg and the commander, realizing they couldn't rule out the possibility of guns being fired, feared for the safety of the civilians. They forbade the news helicopter landing until authorized to do so.

Being in a private helicopter, they were unable to monitor the military radio traffic. The cameraman taped madly not wanting to miss any piece of action. They had no idea what they were observing. Finally, they were allowed to set down.

Jay took in everything moving on the scene. He was eager to talk with Gregg to see what it all meant. Not wanting to interfere, he anxiously waited by the chopper.

Bob Gregg and the commander decided there was no need to continue to be at the site. One thing was clear, Killian would not be back.

The special antiterrorist squad climbed back into the chopper as the blades started their rhythmic thumping. Bob Gregg quickly walked over to Jay where he stood by his station's copter.

"They got away. Tough luck," said Jay, not knowing what else to say.

"Damn!" Gregg muttered as he stomped his foot on the ground. "If that idiot ranger had called headquarters when Killian pulled out of here, we would have had him. We would have had him. Damn it!."

"Apparently the message came just a little too late. How much of a head start does he have?"

"About an hour."

"Now what happens?"

"We sit and hope the highway patrol gets them. How about I hitch a ride back to DC with you? I can fill you in on the way back. We're not going to catch anybody or anything here tonight unless it's pneumonia." Gregg started to get into the station helicopter.

"Wait just a minute," said Jay putting his hand on Gregg's arm keeping him from climbing in. "I don't have authorization for you to ride. You're going to have to find your own return ticket, and it's not in this machine."

"You sonofab-----"

"Okay, okay, as a special favor to you, just this once, I'll let you ride in my chopper." Jay started to laugh.

Gregg shook his head. "You had me going, Dawson. Let's get out of here." The four men climbed into the chopper and headed northeast. The plan was to drop Gregg and Jay in DC at Gregg's office. En route, Jay radioed the story to the station. The pilot would then take the film to the news studio.

The amount of energy radiated by Gregg had the entire craft electrified. Bob Gregg was as wired as Dawson had ever seen him. He was like a contestant in a fight, restless and pumped up.

Dawson tried to calm him by asking questions. "So what's this vehicle look like?"

"It's an Isuzu Trooper. We're unsure of the color because it's covered with dust, but we do have a registration plate. Except, if this guy has any brains, you aren't going to see his number plates. You'll be lucky to get close."

"That narrows it down," mocked Jay. "We're looking for a nondescript colored Isuzu, with unreadable license plates in a sixty mile radius of Skyline Drive."

"Sarcasm I don't need. I wonder if he took his hang glider with him? He must have. It wasn't at the camp. That shit-for-brains ranger!"

"Dawson, let's think about this. One, they plan to make a hit in DC."

"Check."

"Two, they plan to do it with a hang glider."

"Check."

"Three...What's three?" asked Bob Gregg, lost for an answer.

"Three is they do it tonight," guessed Dawson. The other men in the chopper looked at Jay.

"What makes you think tonight?" questioned Gregg, sounding as though the idea was plausible.

"Why not tonight? Killian got the hell out of Dodge and is heading for Tombstone."

"Who or what is his target?"

"Not sure. What's going on tonight, or for that matter, tomorrow night?"

"Don't know. Let's phone security and find out."

"Wait a minute, wait a minute, wait a minute," said Jay shaking his thinking finger again. "Terror is for creating terror. What if there isn't any reason? Why are they doing this? What if this is just purely for the sake of chaos like the Seattle Needle? What if, what if, what if..." his speech trailed off as his thoughts began to race.

Then Bob Gregg picked up on Jay Dawson's train of thought. "What if this is purely for the sake of doing it? Aside from New York and Seattle, what other terrorist attempts have there been in this country?"

"At least none that the government and the media have ever let us know about," interjected Jay. "Like that plane crashing into the White House in '94."

"Exactly. If someone wants to do something really big that won't go ignored, what better job than to assassinate the president of the United States?"

"If you could bomb the White House, that would be even more spectacular."

"How ya' gonna' do it, son?" drawled Bob Gregg.

"The only way you can-----by stealth."

"And maybe with the help of some internal department," Bob Gregg suggested. "Give me the radio. Let's call Secret Service before it's too late." The pilot handed the mike to Gregg.

There was a long pause as Bob Gregg just held the mike in mid air, his mouth hanging open with no sound coming out. "Internal? If it is, who can we trust?" Slowly Bob Gregg handed the mike back to the pilot.

32

"Driving north on Interstate 81 is like driving in any direction on any interstate," thought Eric, "Long and monotonous." It had been nearly an hour of driving since he begrudgingly let Amanda borrow a jacket to wear while she drove her motorcycle. "It's getting cold! Wish I hadn't loaned her my jacket."

As the two vehicles neared Winchester, he decided to stop and take a break. There was no need to rush since Chessie didn't expect them until tomorrow. "Besides," he thought, "Amanda is probably freezing her ass off riding that bike."

Pulling into a parking space at a convenience store, Eric saw that Amanda parked two spaces down. She unbuckled her helmet and shook her hair free from the matted look the helmet had forced it into.

"Christ!" Amanda exclaimed, "I didn't think you'd ever stop. My hands are ice."

"Thought this cold might call for some speedball coffee. It's always too strong in these places, but it's hot and it'll keep you awake."

The clerk behind the counter glanced from the TV screen when the two approached to pay for their coffee.

"Well, isn't that something," the clerk said shaking his head. "Damn army missed catching some international terrorists by this much." He lifted his hand with an inch between his forefinger and thumb.

"Hadn't heard," said Eric in an even tone.

"Yeah, some government dipsticks figure there were some camping down on Skyline Drive. When they flew in, the army found out they left an hour earlier. Pretty good, huh. Day late and dime short. Nothing like the wise use of my tax dollars."

"Yeah, pretty good," said Eric in return handing the clerk money and walked outdoors. Amanda had already returned to her bike and had her helmet on.

"Look, Flash," Killian said, "No more stops until we get to Chessie's. Drive normally. Do nothing to attract attention. We have to assume they have broadcast my plate number through the state. This darkness will work in our favor, but we still need to be careful. Once we get through Winchester, we'll take secondary roads to Leesburg."

Before getting back into the Trooper, Eric broke the license plate light. He looked up at the sky. It was clear. There was no chance for a rain that would wash his camouflage dust from his four-by-four.

Climbing into the truck, Killian got back onto the highway. "Damn it," he muttered pounding the steering wheel. "What went wrong? Did Safran figure it out and make a call? No, she wasn't that good. Something, or more properly, somebody, is that good, very very good."

While in this tense state of mind, he drove to Chessie's. He was greeted outside the outbuilding by Frank.

33

Chessie got up from the kitchen table and walked over to his work area. Picking up a leaflet of papers, he began to page through them, reviewing each timetable thoughtfully.

Amanda and Eric would soon be there. They would go over the layout of the park and run through the plan so every one knew exactly what their job would be.

Earlier that day, Chessie had been to DC and walked the route to compare it to the plan. Some slight adjustments had been necessary due to road work and building renovations.

After a good night's rest, and a day to prepare final details, they would strike.

"After the CCPU claims responsibility for the attack," Chessie mentally reviewed, "Everybody will be scrutinizing

flights to Europe. We shall be disbursed in opposite
directions. Amanda will meet Eric on the Mall after the
attack and will drive to Dahlgren. There they'll take a rented
boat down the Chesapeake to Norfolk to catch a flight to
Mexico." Everything ticked and ticked again inside his
mental checklist, Chessie still walked over to his wall charts
to review his maps for the hundredth time.

He had looked at the map and gone over his plan so
may times he knew every detail of the area. The only
unknown at this point was what may transpire in the capital
area before the mission was executed. He hedged his bet by
taking the walking tour that day. He felt certain that very
little would change and that if it did it would not be
detrimental to the mission.

Chessie stepped back from the boards and bowed his
head. "Don't worry, darlings, tomorrow at this time, all will
be vindicated." He was silent for a moment remembering the
beautiful faces of his wife and son, and the strong characters
of his mother and father. Everything was finally coming
together. Tomorrow night history would be made and the
lives of his family would be avenged.

He was startled out of his reverie by the phone ringing.
He went into the other room to pick it up, but he said
nothing.

An electronic voice on the other end syllabicated.
"The pieces are set. King is on the white square." Then there
was the sound of dead air.

Chessie was startled once again as the door to the
outside opened noisily. Entering the room were Frank,
Amanda and Killian.

"What the devil are you doing here? You're early! A
whole day early!" Exclaimed Chessie. Seeing the look on
Frank's face, Chessie asked, "What's happened?"

"We must execute tonight," stated Frank simply.

"Why?"

The three went into their discourse. At the end of it, Chessie just sat staring at them. After a moment where no one spoke, Chessie finally said, "One phone call please," and excused himself.

Michael Chessie rarely phoned Blankenship. This was an exception. On the other end, Darian Blankenship picked up the phone and said hello.

"Darian, how are you this evening?" inquired Chessie faking interest.

"Michael? I'm...I'm fine. To what pleasure do I owe this call?" Blankenship was concerned, puzzled and anxious all at the same time.

"Well, old friend, you know that chess game we arranged for our friends? Due to some unforeseen business matter that has just arisen, they will have to play it tonight."

"Tonight?!" half choked the secretary of state.

"Yes, sorry to disturb you with such trivial news, but they had a question about the positioning. Will the King still be on the white square?"

There came a silence over the line accented only by anxious breathing. "I'm not sure, Michael. Let me check the journal." Less than a minute lapsed and Blankenship had the response, "Yes, most definitely. The King is on the white square. Most definitely."

"Thank you, my good man, and again, I'm sorry to have disturbed you, but it couldn't be helped."

"N...n...no trouble," Blankenship stuttered, then he regained his composure. "Will I be seeing you at the air show this coming week?"

"I shall be there, eager to bid. Good night, now."

"Yes, good night, Michael."

Chessie smiled, and returned to the other room.

"We move tonight." He left the three and walked outside. The brisk autumn air felt good. He went over to the shed where the explosives were stored. Flipping on the light, he saw the crates where he had left them a few days ago.

Not tomorrow, but tonight, pay back for his family would be
in full.

34

Chessie glanced at his watch. It was 2:30 in the morning. Typical for this time of year, a heavy dew was on the ground and it was cool. "Killian had better be wearing enough warm clothing because it is going to be a cold ride," he thought.

Chessie and Frank had taken enough early morning flights during the last few months. The starting of the engine at this hour should not alarm any of the neighbors. Under the guise of research, Chessie had explained away the early morning flights. This would be just another data gathering flight as far as the community would think. Little did they know what type of data they hoped to gather.

Leesburg is a rural center struggling with the pains of urbanization. Growing into a bedroom community for

Washington professionals, the farms in the area were quickly selling out to the land developers for new housing. With development came complaints of too much noise. After the first few flights, Chessie received a personal visit from the sheriff to investigate the early morning ruckus. After all, those new homeowners voted and the sheriff would like to keep his job.

Explaining the flights as research, the sheriff was pacified and simply asked Chessie to keep the flights to a minimum. Being a long-term resident of Leesburg, the sheriff knew the good old boy farmers, having picked fruit for most of them while he was growing up. He didn't want to disturb the research which might benefit his lifelong buddies. Besides, the farmers also voted.

Chessie was glad he had made the effort to address various social and professional groups in Leesburg such as the Daughters of the American Revolution, because now they wouldn't question this night flight. He walked to the single engine Cessna. Strolling around the plane he inspected the leading edges, landing gears, and hook release. As he climbed into the cockpit he saw Frank and Killian walk to the glider to begin their preparations. He turned on the Cessna's overhead lamp and continued his preflight.

Frank performed his external inspection following the same careful steps as Chessie. "Strangest looking bird, I have ever seen," Frank thought. "Need a damn step ladder to climb into the cockpit of my glider."

Ordinarily, Frank would be able to step down into the glider cockpit to perform his preflight. The special rig under the plane glider, built to allow room for Killian's hang glider, added five feet of height to the normally sleek fuselage.

"Hope Killian said his prayers last night," Frank thought. He still had his doubts about its effectiveness. Inside the cockpit, Frank paid special attention to two levers. The first was the normal tether release-----to ensure it was in the locked position. The other was the customized release installed with the rig which would release the hang glider at the appropriate time. That too was in the locked position.

The rig release had two steps. The first released the plane glider during flight and the plane glider and the hang glider flew in tandem, connected by a cord. This gave the hang glider the altitude necessary to make the trip to the White House as well as the forward momentum needed for the successful flight of any airborne object.

The second, protected by a thumb guard, released the rig from the bottom of the plane glider, and the hang glider would be on its independent way. Releasing the hang glider reduced the drag on the silent plane, and allowed it to land normally, using its one forward wheel.

Killian looked at his hang glider. Realizing that for the first time he was combining two of his greatest loves: hang gliding and fighting the fight for money. Now, if he could just find a way to fit a woman in the hang glider, he could combine his top three favorites.

Looking at the catches which held the hang glider to the rig he made sure the release would not tear his wing, reducing his ability to fly. The hasty tests they did run at the farm and at the Washington Monument successfully released the hang glider.

Killian slowly walked to the front to check the tether that was the connection between Chessie's Cessna and Frank's glider plane. Picking the nylon cord up in his hand he pulled on it hard. The tether held fast, securely held by the lock controlled in the cockpit. The tether being the only thing getting him airborne, Killian had no desire to have it release prematurely. A premature release before they attained sufficient height would send Frank's glider and him back to the earth as one unit. Frank would release the hang glider to save his own hide and to land safely. With insufficient altitude, Killian's landing, if that was what you would call it, would probably be his last. He checked the time delay device on the warhead to ensure his safe clearance before the explosion.

Holding the tether he let it slide through his hand as he walked toward the Cessna. There was a slight slack in the cord which would need to be taken up before take off.

Frank trailed Killian by ten feet also inspecting the cord as he walked. He joined Chessie and Killian who were standing back surveying the contraption of the three flying machines.

"It looks like a good morning to fly: clear skies and cool," said Chessie.

"That may be true for you, but remember thermals is how we survive," Killian replied thrusting a thumb toward Frank.

"Well, with the hot days we have been having the concrete in the city should give you sufficient lift to complete your mission," replied Chessie. "Frank, remember, after you release fly northeast towards Baltimore. You know where to land. I'll meet you."

"I know," said Killian, "I keep flying, ditch the hang glider, and meet Amanda at the theatre where she drives us to a boat waiting on the Potomac. We have been through this plan ten times since we've been here. We're ready, Chessie. Give it a bit of a rest!"

"Plan your work, then work your plan," reminded Chessie with a scowl.

The three men walked back to the shed containing the missiles. Chessie and Killian lifted a box containing the air to ground missile. Killian placed it on his shoulder and walked back out to the hand glider. Gingerly, he removed the custom made launcher from the box and snapped it in the center of the hang glider's control bar. "Ready for the hunt," Killian sneered.

Chessie began again. "The living quarters are on the second floor, left hand corner. Now remember you do not have to put the missile through the window. This thing contains enough explosive that if you get close, it will do the same job as flying it up Glenelly's ass."

"That makes eleven times," Killian muttered.

Frank climbed into the glider and lowered the canopy and hit the switches. The interior instruments glowed red.

Killian put on his helmet and pulled the chin strap tight. The missile tube was fastened to the hang glider using a tripod mount. The center of the tube was mounted to the hang glider and acted as a swivel point until the other two legs were tightened to the center bar of the hang glider. One leg fastened to the leading edge of the hang glider while the other fastened to the trailing edge. Killian rechecked the missile launcher so all he had to do was be on line with the White House when he fired the missile.

He eased himself into the harness and fastened the belts which made him one with the hang glider, his chest barely twelve inches off the ground. Flexing his ankle, he could feel the ground with the toe of his boot.

Chessie climbed into the cockpit of the Cessna and turned the engine over. It caught and sputtered into a rhythmic hum, ready to take off. Easing the Cessna forward, the nylon cord tightened. The single engine struggled against the additional weight of the glider behind him. Slowly, both planes rolled forward.

The glider started to roll with a lurch. Killian thought aloud, "I'll be glad when this thing gets airborne. If we wait too much longer I'm going to become claustrophobic."

The plane began to gain speed as it rolled down the field. The glider trailing silently behind had stabilized as it was now riding smoothly on the wheels of the rig. The Cessna took off and the glider followed like an obedient child.

"Christ," thought Frank, "That rig is really weighing me down. Without it I would have been off the ground twenty-five feet ago."

Killian breathed a sigh of relief as the air beneath him increased. With his right hand he made a few last minute adjustments to the missile launcher. The strange combination of planes circled around and flew east.

"This is a relatively simple plan," thought Chessie. "But it has a few million variables. What if the glider did not have the lift it needed to release the hang glider and get to Baltimore? What if Killian overshot his target?" He continued to ponder as he flew the Cessna towards Bethesda.

The threesome was able to see Bethesda ten minutes before they flew over it. The combination of interstates, government and commercial buildings made it glow in the early morning. As they flew over the eastern boundary of the city, Chessie squeezed the button on his microphone twice to let Frank know he was ready to release. An echoing double click came back over Chessie's receiver confirming Frank was also ready.

Three seconds later, the pitch of the Cessna's engine changed. No longer towing the added weight of the glider, it was not working as hard. Chessie gently banked the plane northwest.

The glider dipped slightly as the resistance of the air and the weight of the glider became a flight factor. Frank gently eased the nose of the plane upward and started a soft turn to the south. The rolling countryside, unseen below, gave the glider some lift.

Although dark, Frank and Killian were able to make out reflections on the Potomac River one thousand feet below them and to the southwest. Both had their fingers crossed that no other aircraft would be in their space.

Frank continued to work the air currents trying to maintain his altitude. Under the best conditions, night flying is difficult for a glider. Without the sun there are few thermal currents radiating from the earth's surface. The heated earth created massive updrafts enabling gliders to stay airborne sometimes for hours, much like the way eagles and hawks glide effortlessly through the sky.

Without the help of the sun, Frank tried to stay away from the river. Water is cooler than the ground, giving no chance of an updraft. Frank was able to nurse the air currents directed by the sides of the river valley as the currents were propelled skyward by the slope of the valley floor. As he neared Washington, Frank was able to take advantage of some of the heat radiated by the concrete surfaces.

As they flew over Georgetown, Frank was at eleven hundred feet. According to plan, he was to begin flying over the river at this point. Paralleling the river was easy, although dangerous. If he could just maintain this altitude for another three quarters of a mile, he would release Killian and begin his escape.

Although Killian was protected from the harsh winds, his hands and feet were becoming numb. Flying at eleven hundred feet being carried by a noiseless bird was much different than soaring at eleven hundred feet on his own. Because he was being carried, Killian had nothing to do. The flight to this point was so boring he felt he could take a nap. He flexed his fingers and toes trying to increase the circulation. He could not afford to have stiff fingers in the next ten minutes.

Killian was flying over Georgetown and knew they would soon be over Interstate 66. A few minutes longer and he would be active and again in control.

In the distance he could see the lights along the bridge. There was hardly any traffic. The bridge connected Washington D.C. with Arlington Cemetery in northern Virginia.

As the craft neared the bridge, Frank squeezed the button on his microphone to signal Killian he would release in thirty seconds. Killian checked his helmet down on his head and pulled the chin strap tight for good measure. He glanced up at the releasing mechanism to make sure there would be no chance of fouling when the hang glider separated itself from the glider. Lastly he checked the missile.

The microphone button clicked in Killian's ear. They were crossing the Arlington Bridge.

Five...four...three...two...one. Killian heard the metal release strain under his weight. In a second he was free beneath the glider plane. The plane continued its gliding path down river. With a little luck Frank would make it to a field near Baltimore.

Killian and his hang glider began to shift and to slow. Shifting his weight, Killian turned his glider to the east. His flight line was easy to follow: the Kennedy Center, then straight across E Street to pass the White House on his left. On his right there was the Mall as L'Enfant had envisioned it, modeled after the wondrous promenades of Paris, France: the Lincoln Memorial, the reflecting pool, the Washington Monument and the Capital. In the early morning it was not difficult to see these monuments to men, by men, awash with light.

Killian's fingers were getting back to normal now that he had something to do. He was able to flex them and maneuver his wing as he needed.

The angle of descent had been predetermined and factored into the positioning of the missile's tripod mounting. If Killian was capable of keeping an etched horizontal line on the face of his goggles, bisecting the bedroom window, the missile would be adequately aimed to insure the destruction of the private quarters of the White House.

The sighting technique was copied from NASA and was similar to the technique used to align the Apollo spacecraft for reentry. Misalignment in space would send the spacecraft bouncing off the atmosphere never to be seen again. Misalignment now would send his missile off target and waste much good effort and planning. The approach to the White House was over an open field bisected by a few roads. The smooth surface coupled with the lack of concrete allowed for a slow graceful descent. As Killian flew over the ellipse he had his target in sight.

35

"That makes the fifth time I've phoned, and all I get is their voice mail." Bob Gregg slammed the phone down in disgust. "Where are they at two in the morning?"

"Doesn't Secret Service have another line? Can you raise them some other way?" Jay Dawson asked hoping to find an alternative approach.

"Yeah, sure, I'll see if anyone's sorting today's mail," retorted Gregg.

"Sarcasm we don't need," Dawson repeated Greg's earlier advice.

"Okay, okay. I can't just sit here. I'm driving over to the White House and knock on the front door. Maybe I'll get someone's attention that way. Do you want to come?"

"Thanks, no. I'm tired. It's frustrating not being able to do anything. I'm going to jog back to the hotel. Phone me if anything breaks."

"What hotel? You're welcome to sleep on my office couch."

"Thanks, but the station maintains a room at the Holiday Inn. I'll be there if you want me. See you later."

Both men left the building at the same time. Jay Dawson began his jog across the mall, while Robert Gregg went to the parking garage to get his van.

It was 2:30 a.m. and both men could not shake the feeling of impending doom. Gregg hoped he could get an answer more quickly to his questions if he went directly to the front gate. Dawson hoped he could get an answer more quickly by jogging his body and his brain. Both men got answers.

Jay left the Justice Department Building and headed west toward the Washington Monument. Turning south along 15th Street, he approached the brightness of the structure. It was the capital's punctuation mark, a giant exclamation point. All the monuments of the city were lit. "What grandeur," Jay thought. "It serves as an illusion so you don't see life's reality under your nose. Real life is that homeless person sleeping on the steam vent over there, trying to keep warm." He cut east toward the Mall when he reached the front of the monument. He hoped he wouldn't trip over any homeless bodies along the gravel path.

The mall was well lit and the path easily seen, so he released the thought of tripping over someone. Jogging purposely towards a warm bed, Dawson tried to calm his mind. His sites focused ahead, he could make out the silhouette of a woman pacing in front of a small van. Adjusting his stride, he maintained his distance from the figure giving himself ample time to appreciate yet another attractive illusion. Without the physical form, for all he knew, the shadow could have had the head of Medusa. She had no substance.

He slowed to walk in unison behind the person. His reporter instincts noticed little details about the woman, her gait, her hair, her demeanor. In the dim light her familiarity struck him like a blow to the solar plexus. It couldn't be! But then, why not?

He came to a dead stop in his walk. He knew he shouldn't stop, but this familiarity was too big to ignore.

"Amanda?" called Jay to the shadow in shock and disbelief.

The figure pivoted as if on a spindle.

"Yeah, what?"

"Remember me, the guy you framed for murder? What are you doing here?" What a stupid question. He knew why she was here. Maybe the stupid question had some intelligence, though because if she guessed what he knew, his life could come to an abrupt DC end.

"I've taken up with the homeless. What's it to you?" she quipped.

"I can't believe I'm actually going to get to ask you this question. Why did you frame me?"

"You were there. You were easy. It was necessary," she said with harshness. Then she softened slightly. "It's best if you ignore me and continue walking." Then in a commanding tone, "Leave the Mall. Now."

"Amanda, you know I can't do that," he couldn't stop blurting out. "The authorities are searching for you. They know what you and your group are up to." He gestured widely. "Hell, Amanda, they just missed you last night on the Parkway. Five minutes earlier and they would have had your ass along with Killian's."

Hearing this from Dawson, shook Amanda. They had tried to play their cards close to the chest. If a civilian knew where they stayed and who some of the conspirators were, what did the authorities know?

"Jay, I wish you had taken my advice and not changed. You have become one of those anal types. You have lost the naivete I found so appealing."

"Yeah, well, let me tell you. Getting arrested for murder kinda strips you of your naivete. I thought you and I shared a few laughs and we were becoming friends."

"You thought wrong. You were just a patsy. You so-called free thinkers believe you have all the answers to the world problems. Let me tell you. The world is sick. It's decaying and if you don't grab your piece you'll be left clutching air."

"So you and your terrorist friends decide rather than go mainstream you'll kill and maim society, attempting to influence through force, terrorism and anarchy. Is that it, Amanda? Does that sum up your creed?"

Shahey responded by pulling a 9mm pistol from behind her, and leveled it at Dawson's chest. "Jay, I really am sorry."

A brilliant illumination lit the night sky, seconds before a tremendous explosion ripped the dark quiet of the city.

It was the White House.

Looking toward the noise, they saw an orange flame radiating from a central fireball annihilating the early morning darkness. In that moment of distraction, Dawson lunged toward Amanda.

Amanda saw the movement and fired.

Dawson felt a searing pain in his left shoulder. The impact of the shot sent his left shoulder back and began to spin him around in the direction of the ground. His forward momentum drove his right shoulder into Amanda's chest. This propelled Amanda backwards and down. Falling, she hit her head on the truck and the gun fell to the ground a couple feet away. Amanda was stunned, but not knocked out. Gasping, she struggled to catch her breath. Jay was slow to rise, agonized by the bullet in his shoulder. Intense pain, like molten steel, tore in all directions from his shoulder. His left arm was useless. He rolled off Amanda. She labored to her hands and knees. The blow to her chest had driven the wind from her lungs. Gasping, she groped for the gun. The gun was directly in front of Dawson. He picked it up with his right hand and struggled to his feet.

Amanda felt the muzzle of the gun in the nape of her neck. She heard the click of the hammer as it was pulled into place. She froze. Dawson increased the pressure on the back of her head and forced her to· the ground. "Don't move. Don't talk. Don't flinch a fucking muscle," he growled through clenched teeth.

"But, Jay," she almost sounded sweet.

"I have more than a gun. I have sensory overload. You just shot me. You have just killed my president. You tried to frame me for a murder you committed, and now you and your tattoos are on the receiving end of a pistol. I am shot, sore, and bleeding. Right now I need a reason to allow you to live. If I kill you, we're equals. However, as I lose blood I feel muscle spasms starting to creep over my body," Jay could not stop the flow of his talk any more than he could stop the flow of his blood. "I have no control and may at any time suffer a severe spasm in my hand. If that occurs, I am afraid I might shoot you. The more you move the more frequent the spasms." He was operating on reserve energy. His teeth began to clatter. "If that occurs I am afraid I might shoot you, accidentally. If you flinch a muscle and attempt to get up, a massive spasm may wrack my entire body. Do you understand?" Amanda Shahey understood and did not move. "How do I fall into these things?" Jay slurred.

Sirens were everywhere. Sirens are not unusual in DC. The combination of usual emergency traffic coupled with the police escorts serve to anaesthetize frequent visitors to Washington. But nobody could fathom the number and volume of sirens after the explosion at the White House.

Dawson had a unique seat to watch the happenings. The sky above the White House glowed orange, while the vicinity around the White House flashed in rotating sequences of red, white and blue. Police, fire departments, secret service, SWAT teams and military intelligence personnel were everywhere.

He felt the creeping effects of shock through his body. Despite the chill in the air he was sweating. He knew he was not up to walking for help and might soon lose consciousness. He was hoping a SWAT team would relieve him of Amanda before he passed out.

In the distance Jay made out two spots of light slowly coming towards him. The vehicle was driving slowly down the center of the mall panning two searchlights to its right and left. When the vehicle got within a hundred feet of Dawson and his prisoner, the spotlights converged and blinded them.

From behind the lights a loud and brusque voice commanded, "You are in a restricted area. You must evacuate immediately."

Dawson did not move. Dawson could not move. He wanted to stand but his body was ignoring his commands. Slowly he raised his arm with the gun clenched in it. He was amazed that at a hundred feet he was clearly able to make out the sound of five guns chambering a round.

Police converging on the couple could just make out the bloodstained Justice Department clearance badge on Dawson's jacket. They immediately shifted their attention to the woman on the ground. In semi-delirium, Jay managed to utter the word terrorist, and then blacked out.

36

President Thomas Glenelly could not sleep. He found himself pacing his bedroom at two in the morning. "Since I can't sleep, let's see if I can slip by my guards out to the rose garden," he thought. Quietly, he opened his door. The guards were conversing at the other end of the hall. He left the door open, went back into his bedroom, and went through the door into his adjoining study.

Quietly, he opened that door just enough to get out. The opened door from his bedroom blocked the view of the study door. He slipped undetected into the hall, hugged the wall and made it to the stairwell. "The world can fall asleep, but never my body guards." He noticed that there was a reduction in the numbers as he went to the east wing. "Family's vacationing in the Caribbean. Maybe that's why there aren't so many." Glenelly chuckled to himself. "I wonder if they are any less vigilant." He stepped noiselessly along.

As he approached the east wing he paused at the doors leading to the rose garden. "There he is, the guard of the garden. How do I get by him unseen?" The President didn't have to wonder. The guard had received a call on his walkie talkie and was coming into the White House. Glenelly stepped behind a large plant that was there. The guard walked passed him. Thomas Glenelly stepped into the garden, still undetected.

Ever since the election, he had always wanted to shake his protectors. He had succeeded a few times before, but a feeling of unease came over him. Now that his human shields were removed, he felt vulnerable. He was unable to explain this feeling.

Walking amongst the rose bushes, he headed for the arbor. In this alcove he felt a weight lift from his shoulders. Funny how rose gardens seemed to have this temporary effect on him. He was pleased that the guard had not seen him, but he couldn't shake the feeling of impending doom.

Then a sound, like the fluttering of a kite held taut in the wind, caught his attention. Looking in that direction he witnessed a black pterodactyl-like shape glide against the dark grey sky of early morning. "What the hell is that?" he said aloud.

It may have been two in the morning, but he knew he was fully awake. What the hell was flying here? Open mouthed he saw the shape pass by, then a flash as something sped from it, shattering the window of the bedroom he had just minutes ago so cleverly left undetected.

Five seconds later, a tremendous explosion ripped through the presidential residence.

"Jesus! Am I in the Twilight Zone?"

Knowing he was in danger, all his instincts and reactions functioned automatically. He started running toward

Executive Avenue. Sirens in the distance, the fire's heat on his back, reeling, he looked over his shoulder. The second story of the White House was ablaze. His bedroom and study were ablaze. His mind was numb, but some power was moving his legs.

Nearing the corner of the Treasury Building, he saw an unmarked van. From out of no where someone was at his side, taking his arm, guiding him toward that vehicle. A wave of nausea hit him.

"Mr. President, I'm with ATI," Bob Gregg shouted flashing his ID card. "You're in terrible danger. Come with me." Totally disorientated, the President, silent and shaken, got into the van.

"Get down," said Gregg. "You don't want to be seen." The van went around the block and headed toward the northwest sector of DC, and away from the converging activity in the White House Area.

37

Eric Killian was quite pleased with himself. He could not believe the ease with which the missile had been launched. "State of the art, indeed," he thought. As he made his descent.

He had been released from the glider above the Kennedy Center. He used the westerly coming from the Potomac River to work toward the White House. The calculations had been figured correctly, and it put him level with the second story windows as he passed in front of it just over the ellipse.

His aim had been faultless. The missile had entered the designated window, just as planned. There was a delayed detonation, thank God it worked, so that he could be well out of the way when it exploded. Practicing with the missiles in the mountains helped him to correct for the kick from the firing.

Targeting the Washington Monument was child's play, except that he had been too high. Somehow the concrete around the monument had held enough heat from the day, to create an updraft. When the lift took him by surprise, the sack he carried to compensate for the weight of the missile, had to be released in order to keep from crashing.

Setting down in the Mall afterwards was a piece of cake. A middle of the night landing between the museums was an excellent choice, as no one was about at the time. He was very surprised, though, at the quick reaction of the rangers. He didn't think the sack would be found until daylight. That foul up lead to more practice in the mountains.

Chessie had intercepted him in the van between Madison and Jefferson Streets. He was able to disassemble the glider and pack it away in the dark. Black on black, in the dark, is very difficult to discern. It's even harder when you feel you're invisible, which the hang glider was to radar.

As the past episode flashed through his mind, he master handled the glider eastward on E Street. He was to land on the building directly across from the monument for Count Pulaski, in Freedom Park. Amanda would be waiting for him in a van across from the Warner Theatre. He heard the explosion, and took great delight in a job well done. He didn't have to look back to see if he was on target. He knew he was on target and that the President of the United States, the Right Honorable Mr. Thomas Glenelly, had been sent on his way to meet his Maker.

He smiled tensely. Everything had come together even though pushed to fly a day early. All this was meant to take place as it had. There were even enough thermals available from the streets and walkways to give the hang glider sufficient lift to land on top of the designated building.

Another plan executed to precision. Yes, that Chessie sure knows how to put a plan together.

As he began to drop to the building top, Killian's eyes opened wide in disbelief. It was too late to maneuver out of the way.

"Noooooooo," he shouted as he landed directly impaled on the antenna extension of a satellite dish. It had been installed after Chessie's reconnaissance. The dish had been placed there that day for installation.

38

When the President got into the van with Bob Gregg, they drove off toward northwest DC, out of range of the converging activity.

"Here, put on this hat and jacket. Slouch in the seat and look as undignified as possible," ordered Gregg giving him a ball cap and windbreaker that he had in the vehicle.

"What the hell's going on? You're ATI? How'd you guys let this happen?"

"Yeah, I'm Bob Gregg, ATI, but one of the goodies. Some of us knew about this hit, but there are baddies who let it happen."

"How do I know you're one of the goodies?"

"The way I see it, you really don't have much choice but to take my word for it, Mr. President."

"Where are you taking me?"

"Somewhere safe."

"Which is?"

"Right under their noses here in DC."

"Are you crazy?"

"I'm at my best when I'm crazy. It's what keeps me from going insane," rationalized Gregg.

The van circled westward around the zoo taking the long way to Georgetown, across the Potomac to the Arlington Cemetery, then took a back approach to the Lincoln Memorial. This took a half hour. It gave Bob Gregg time to phone ahead to his network for the President's safe accommodation. He had a place in mind ever since he picked him up on the White House lawn. The sky was no longer a bright orange from the burning of the White House, but people were lining the streets, although it was four o'clock in the morning.

"Mr. President, I have some rather dependable friends, although scruffy looking. They will meet you on the Potomac Parkway Bridge. They are watching for me, and know that you are with me. Please listen to them, and trust them. I will tell you now that they are enlisted in the ranks of the homeless, and are experts about the best places to stay off the beaten track in this city. Trust them."

"But---"

"Here's where you get out." At that, the door on the passenger side was opened and two wiry but strong men pulled the President from his seat. Gregg drove away before the door could be closed.

Most of the people on the street at this hour were near the White House watching the fire. If anyone had noticed this curbside abduction, no one let on. After all it was only two vagrants supporting another homeless drunk.

Making their way across the street, the three walked to the back of the Lincoln Monument.

"Would you mind telling me where the hell you're taking me?"

"We're taking you to where the homeless, tempest tossed have been laying their heads for the last several years."

"Where's that?"

"Honest Abe has been brooding over us, and he's become the perfect protector."

The rhododendrons provided a good cover as the men circled their way around the south side of the monument. They came out near the lower level where an entrance lead to the chronicles of the construction of the monument. Although the lights were out, the scruffy body guards knew exactly where they were going.

"Why are we stopping here?" asked the President when the little group came to a halt just ten feet inside.

"We are at the entrance to your temporary new home, Sir." At that he pressed the arm of the bench that was there and it moved outward quite easily. A dim glow could be seen beyond this entry.

"Follow me, Mr. President," instructed one of the men.

"These are the catacombs!" exclaimed Glenelly with a bit of excitement in his voice. "I've never been down here before. Say," he began suspiciously, "didn't they find asbestos down here some years ago?"

"Yes, they did."

"Then why are you down here?"

"Somehow we find it safer to be with the asbestos, than take our chances on some doorway."

As they descended the steps, the glow became brighter. The columns supporting the monument were enormous. The glow was created by the fires from campsites. It was like a little medieval village. The top of the underneath part of the memorial had to be fifty feet high. The smoke, if there was any, rose to that height and found its way out. All fires were extinguished at six in the morning, when the rangers came around and checked the monuments.

Down in this recess, it was warm and an atmosphere of an organized hospice permeated. There was a set of rules and they were enforced. Everyone had to get fresh air and daylight daily. There were no exceptions. The ill were taken to churches or clinics. There was an unspoken rule of care for the elderly and the infirmed. The President was impressed.

"Mr. President, this isn't what you're used to, but if you abide by our rules, no one will find you here."

Just a few of the park rangers not only knew of this shelter, but they unofficially helped maintain the vast network of people and help sort the riff from the raff. None of them knew when they would be left homeless and have to take advantage of the hospitality extended here.

"How long will I have to stay?"

"Until Bob Gregg can get to the bottom of this conspiracy. I'm sure you'll agree that traveling incognito is the best thing to do under the circumstances."

"It's nearly five a.m. Get some sleep, Mr. Glenelly. You're going to have a busy day of it tomorrow. Ben here will show you to your bedroll."

"Sleep? but I have a million questions. First..." for the first time in his life he saw the depths to which middle class America had fallen, or as he was soon to discover, been pushed. "...first, why are there so many homeless? I heard it was bad here in Washington, but this isn't just bad, it's epidemic. How did all this happen? Are the other American cities like this? This is not drunk and disorderly. This is organized. I'm out of touch. I'm the President, surely I can be of some help here."

"Mr. President, with all due respect, you're dead. If the world hasn't heard, it will real soon. There ain't nothin' a dead president can do. Look how much you did while you were alive."

"Mr. President, haven't you seen any of the television documentaries on the homeless?"

"No, I missed them."

"Too bad. It would have given a person like you a lot of insight. Now, my suggestion is that you sleep on it. It's a very big problem, and it won't get solved tonight. Good night, Mr. President," said the man walking away.

Thomas Glenelly was dumbfounded. He was overwhelmed by the events of the last hour as well as by his surroundings. "Homeless, tempest tossed, indeed," he mumbled running his hands hopelessly through his hair.

39

"You read the report. There's no trace of his body. It was totally obliterated along with his bedroom and study," groaned one of the ATI staff. "I need some coffee. We've been at it for over five hours."

"I suppose you're right. Where else would he have been at three in the morning but in his bedroom? Still there wasn't a shred of anything." The second member of staff was less convinced of the President's death.

"Jesus, that hang glider guy knew what he was doing. Pity he didn't see the dish, or else we'd be having a little fun with him right now."

"They said the bomb landed directly where his bed was. Since there was no shred, as you say, of his bed, then it is reasonable to assume he went into oblivion along with it."

"That hit must have been state of the art ordnance," said the second man shaking his head marveling. "Two rooms were demolished and only smoke and water damage to the others. Amazing."

"No, I'd say lucky."

"How do you mean lucky?"

"The fire department responded so quickly, nothing happened to the rest of the White House."

Smiling he said, "I'd say lucky was having a black man as vice president when the president dies. How else would a Black get into office in 1998?"

* * *

Judson Kershaw took the oath of office of the President of the United States two days after the attack on the presidential residence. He had risen in popularity in the last few years as a crusader for the lower class working and homeless, most of whom were black. He was a popular lay person in his church in South Carolina. His charismatic personality and charm helped get much legislation passed to help the less privileged. He was seen as having a great deal of influence.

When Thomas Glenelly announced his candidacy for the 1996 election, he chose Kershaw as his running mate. This political maneuver was brilliant although radical. Brilliant because Kershaw carried the black votes in the country as well as those of the lower economic classes. Radical because a black man had never been on the ticket. Glenelly, a self-made millionaire, read his market well. Although not the most popular choice in his own party, they backed him because he held the winning combination.

All politicians put their best face forward and so it was with Glenelly and Kershaw. Glenelly was all business and gruffness and Kershaw was charm and wit. Outwardly they appeared to make a good team, but in reality Glenelly held some racial prejudices and Kershaw was in it for the glory.

40

"Mr. President. Mr. President. Wake up we need to talk." Scared to move a muscle, Thomas Glenelly slowly opened his eyes. He wasn't sure where he was or who was with him.

"Mr. President, I am Robert Gregg. We met last night, remember? We had uncovered a plot to assassinate you and to undermine the world order. That little party thrown at your window was the culmination of terrorist efforts.

Glenelly listened cautiously. He was still alive, he reminded himself. Gregg related the story which ATI had pieced together. How the terrorists got into the country, where they trained, how they accomplished the attack, and to a limited degree, to what extent the plot had risen within the government.

"You are presently in the hands of these people you see around you. They are homeless, but they are good. They've just had a bit of bad luck. They have agreed to protect you until I tell them it's all right for you to come out."

Finding his voice, the President responded. "So where am I really? Is this truly beneath the Memorial?"

"Sir, you are a pillar of society, a great leader, and an elder spokesman," Gregg said with a cheeky grin. "But we won't hold that against you. It is fitting you are being kept hidden beneath the Lincoln Memorial."

"A pillar of society, eh?" echoed Glenelly looking up at the support columns for Lincoln.

"It isn't much, chilly dirt floors and all, but it is dry and away from the throngs of Washington. Most people don't know this place even exists."

"As you stated earlier, Mr. Gregg, I haven't any choice."

"We need to keep you here until we finish tracking down all the conspirators. We have reason to believe this goes to the highest levels, possibly just short of your office."

"That's impossible!" exclaimed Glenelly. "I have loyal people working for me."

"Sir, that is true. It appears the majority of your staff may not be involved. In fact it is possible none of your staff is involved at all."

The President stood up, walked and felt the firmness of one of the pillars. "Someone's out to get me. That's certain." He turned and looked Gregg straight in the eye. He thought, "It's not you, Robert Gregg, and it's not this lot of homeless people. Just who the hell is it?"

He came back to his bedroll. "Well," he said, shaking his head, "what you've told me is either the greatest lie ever concocted or the truth. Right now I'm leaning towards the truth."

"Mr. President, we will keep you in hiding until it is prudent to bring you out. There will be activities occurring which you may take exception to.   One is your family's reaction. We can not tell them you are alive."

"You must...I will not allow..."

"No, Sir, if the conspirators are to believe you are dead, your family's reaction must be genuine. We will do everything we can to explain this to them afterward, but I believe they will understand as the events unfold."

"Events? What events?"

Gregg ignored this and went on.   "Kershaw will be sworn in as President shortly. I do not even want to think of the constitutional issues to be addressed here; however, following the declaration of the President's death, his taking office may help our investigation."

"That conniving son of a bitch has always wanted the oval office. How will his being President help...You don't mean to tell me he's involved in this some way? He may be shallow and manipulative, but he is not a killer."

"Right now we are not sure who is involved. All I am saying is, by his taking office, the conspirators may relax and not be quite so attentive. The assassins are probably well away from here. It's the ring leaders that we need and we must have them believing that you are dead and gone."

41

The Vice President was seated at the desk in the Oval Office. Although, not officially president until the swearing in ceremony of tomorrow, Judson Kershaw was performing the job.

The nation was amazed at how gracious and understated the former vice president behaved, now that his role had changed. It was almost as though he had been born to the part.

The secretary of state stood behind the accidental president's chair looking over his shoulder at three documents. The first, a non competitive agreement for arms trade worldwide between the US and the Russian States, the very signing of which would make both men wealthy beyond their

dreams.   Both the arms manufacturers and the Russian
government were helping to line their pockets.

The second document was an amnesty treaty with
Sadam Hussein.   The UN would unilaterally call off all
retaliatory actions and allow Sadam to act independently
with his neighboring countries and allow him to trade with
the US which opened up the oil and the arms market. This,
too, was not without its monetary rewards.

A fraction of these, labeled fines, would go into the US
Treasury.   The balance would be wired to previously
arranged Swiss accounts.

The third document provided support to Northern Ireland's CCPU. The treaty promised whatever it would take to
keep Northern Ireland part of Great Britain. This document
was the only one of the three not embroidered with monetary
gain.

"Signing those documents, Sir, will be opening
Pandora's Box," President Kershaw puzzled.

"Perhaps, in fighting fire with fire, the forces will
eventually extinguish each other. In the meantime, there is
no reason why we can't gain from it, is there?"

"Blankenship, how long do you think these secret
documents are going to remain secret? How long do you
think it will take before people will start to figure it out?"

"Mr. President, The American public is putty in our
hands. It will believe we are doing everything possible to
overcome these evils. It will believe anything it is told to
believe. The media will see to that. It will continue to carry
out the job they know so well because they know who really
butters their bread.

"The CIA and the KGB will be back in business as will
our friends in Northern Ireland. The Muslims will be free to
reek havoc with their parts of the world, and you and I and a
few select others will be reaping the benefits of all the lovely
chaos."

"I like to make a buck just like the next guy. It's just that these actions are mega-big. How long can we, or the world, last?"

"The world has withstood worse. Mr. President, I detect a note of reluctance. Do you want out?" Blankenship asked cuttingly.

"No, Mr. Secretary."

"Good," said the secretary of state without any humor, "Then I won't have to kill you. We have analyzed these documents thoroughly. With your legal eye and my dazzling world political savvy, we have thought of every possible loophole. Nothing can touch us now."

"God, this is big," Kershaw stated overawed. His hands shook as he took the pen.

"Do it!" spat out Blankenship. "Put ink to paper, so we can sign, seal and deliver."

42

Judson Kershaw had appeared before television cameras many times before this, but never as the President of the United States. His delivery had always been smooth and with the appearance of a man completely in control, but today, in the recesses of his mind, doubt began to chisel its way through to layers where it had never been previously permitted.

Kershaw was a cautious man, even if his motivations were misguided. He knew exactly why he had been chosen for Thomas Glenelly's running mate. It had everything to do with politics and nothing to do with platform.

This Afro American was excellent at speechifying, but had been frustrated at implementing. He would dearly have loved to put his ideas into action and get legislation passed for the have nots, but he lacked the skills to get around the thwarting. His name was a symbol people rallied behind, and it was from these followers that Kershaw had gained his power, and Glenelly his presidency. The man felt he couldn't be wrong with so many clinging to his every word.

It was precisely at this moment that he lost his perspective. His attention was turned from those who had given him power, to himself. He began to feel that his power was innate. He knew that when he took the oath of office, that he had arrived, that he had been born to a position of power.

The inkling of doubt must be dealt with, and he looked at it full in the face. Once again, he came away misguided. All clues revealed that not one minute bit of the president had been found in the explosion. And it was this fact that caused the gnawing doubt in Kershaw's mind. There should have been some shred of evidence.

Hard facts reality gave way to hard core spirituality. The more he thought about it the more he felt his true destiny was at hand. The fact that Thomas Glenelly had vanished, whether or not it could be explained scientifically, was the miracle that would catapult him there. As the time drew near for the press conference, the gnawing of little doubts had ceased.

The papers were ablaze with anticipation of the newly sworn in President's address to the joint session of Congress. Addresses to joint sessions are infrequent but not rare. The forum is used annually for the State of the Union address and periodically used for the announcement of new presidential initiatives or programs.

The papers had speculated for the past week who President Kershaw was going to announce as his Vice Presidential nominee. Secretary of State Blankenship was the early favorite, but others had also been mentioned.

The House Chamber, the larger of the two chambers, had been meticulously cleaned under the watchful eye of

countless Secret Service agents. After the CCPU claimed
responsibility for the assassination of the president, the Secret
Service was taking no chances for this public address. Like
the papers, the public placed a great deal of blame on the
shoulders of this government agency for the assassination of
President Glenelly, popular despite his shortcomings.

The Secret Service had been named as the subject of no
less than ten investigations announced immediately after the
successfully spectacular assassination. The politicians were
nothing if not expedient at ordering investigations, so long as
they are not the subject of the probes. The television time
provided to the committee members would ensure reelection
for most of them. There is no better forum to show the
constituencies back home how informed and responsive their
elected officials are.

After President Kershaw had announced his desire to
address a joint session of Congress, concerns were voiced
about having so many of the nations leaders gathered in one
place. This was compounded by the embarrassment of
having no suspects in custody other than the corpse of Eric
Killian, found impaled on the probe of a satellite dish atop a
neighboring building. There had been no formal admission
by Shahey of a conspiracy, but it was obvious the nature of
the attack required more than two individuals.

If the assassins could plan and execute such a devious
plan to attack the White House, what would prevent them
from ordering a second attack during the speech. The
world's intelligence network didn't know where Blackhawk
was. There was no evidence he was connected, but there
were strong suspicions he was instrumental. The Secret
Service had necessarily joined forces with the military and
the rest of the intelligence community to provide protection
during the evening.

Additional radar had been placed on the tops of
government buildings. They had also been equipped with

missiles to shoot at anything that came within the prohibited air space.

Under the direction of the Secret Service the maintenance crew normally assigned to the janitorial duties in the House Chamber was replaced. Using random selection, they took one member from other cleaning crews assigned to the Capital. The cleaning staff was divided into teams of three and were assigned one Secret Service person per team.

The other agencies actively taking part in this undercover investigation, other than ATI, were the Central Intelligence Agency, Defense Intelligence Agency, National Security Agency, Federal Bureau of Investigation and the Department of Energy.

Each janitor was searched going into and coming out of the chamber. Bomb sniffing dogs were in evidence during the preparation process. Nothing foreign was going to be placed into the chamber today.

Members of both houses began arriving an hour before the address was scheduled to begin. The capital building, beautiful under normal circumstances was aglow with television lights and added security lighting.

Intelligence agents milled around the grounds and held look alike news cameras taking video tape of the crowds gathering outside the building. Should anything happen tonight they would have miles of tape of the crowd to scour for suspects. Military helicopters circled noisily overhead.

By ten minutes of eight, all members of Congress, the Supreme Court, the Military Joint Chiefs of Staff, and the President's Cabinet had entered the chamber. The television cameras made periodic sweeps of the room showing and labeling various powerful attendees for the watching constituents. Meanwhile, anchor persons reported and speculated upon the content of the President's message.

The reporters were all seated. Cameras were at the ready. Microphones were planted like stakes in a garden. The American public was relaxing into its easy chairs to watch the new president make his first public address. The mood was mixed. Solemn yet anticipatory, an understated excitement was felt by skeptics, cynics, backers and believers.

Promptly at eight o'clock, the sergeant at arms of the House of Representatives walked down the center aisle and announced, "Ladies and gentlemen, the President of the United States of America."

One thousand dignitaries, as if by remote control, stood and erupted into simultaneous applause. Judson Kershaw, the consummate politician, started his purposeful walk down the aisle stopping periodically to shake hands with prechosen and strategically placed loyal party members. Taking a full minute and a half to negotiate the walk from the rear of the chamber to the podium, Kershaw basked in the spotlight. "Finally out of the shadows and into the light," he thought.

The President walked behind the podium and placed his sheaf of papers on it. Turning around, he shook hands with the Speaker of the House. The seat next to the Speaker, reserved for the Vice President of the United States was vacant. Turning and grasping both sides of the lectern, he looked out over the audience. Taking the opportunity to fully exploit the moment and the free television time. Kershaw glanced around the room and up into the gallery where he found his family. Expertly, and with nonchalance, Kershaw blew his wife and his mother a kiss. Television cameras quickly swung around to show the glowing faces of the two women. "That should be good for a few million votes," he thought.

After several minutes, Judson Kershaw raised his hands and motioned for silence. Slowly the crowd settled into their seats and waited for the speech to begin. Nobody expected this to be overly long or of much substance. As many members described it, "a quick in and out."

"Ladies and gentlemen of Congress, Justices, Joint Chiefs and fellow Americans at home, I am here this evening to make several announcements and to make known my vision of America's role in the world. Before I begin, however, let us take a moment of silence to remember our fallen leader, my predecessor and friend, the late President Thomas Glenelly and his family." Kershaw paused and bowed his head. Waiting a respectful thirty seconds, Kershaw looked up. Casually, he shifted his weight and cleared his throat to let everybody watching know it was once again his turn in the spotlight. "Tomorrow morning, I will place in nomination to the upper chamber of this esteemed governing body, the name of the individual I feel is most capable to assist me in leading our nation into the future. My nominee is an individual who has assisted tremendously in the past years in shaping our relations with other nations, has been active in supporting President Glenelly's cabinet and in the last few mournful days, has personally assisted me through a most difficult transition. I speak, of course, of Secretary of State Darian Blankenship."

All eyes and cameras turned and focused upon the gentleman sitting in the aisle seat near the podium. Fixing his face to register modesty and humbleness, Blankenship tipped his head toward the stage.

The standing ovation and raucous applause was the cover Robert Gregg needed to reach into the chamber and ask the sergeant at arms to step into the hallway. The ovation for Blankenship was predictably lengthy. The applause was allowed for a full three minutes before Mr. Kershaw continued on with his address.

"Secretary Darian Blankenship has a distinguished history of leadership and public service. There is no doubt in my mind his nomination will be ratified quickly by the Senate and placed into the position he can so competently serve. His presence in the White House, and in the world, will provide America with the stature necessary to maintain our position as the world super power.

"Ladies and Gentlemen, in my opening remarks I indicated I would make several announcements and pass along my vision for America. To that end, I am very pleased that I can announce to you, tonight, an agreement which has been finalized over the last few days by myself and with the direct involvement of Vice President Designate Blankenship."

The stunned silence in the room was deafening. The man had not been in the White House a week and had already consummated a treaty without anyone's knowledge. Congressional leadership glanced at one another, shrugged their shoulders and fidgeted in their seats.

"This treaty between the United State of America and our friends the----"

From the rear of the chamber came a loud rapping sound which stopped Kershaw midsentence.   In the electrified silence all heads swung to see who was creating the disturbance. The sergeant at arms was banging the ceremonial scepter firmly on the floor. The action achieved the desired result, undivided attention and focus on the Sergeant at Arms. Even the television cameras focused on the man while the journalists whispered to the people at home of their uncertainty, and just how unusual this was.

The sergeant at arms halted the pounding, glanced around the chamber and for the second time that evening announced in a loud clear voice, "Ladies and gentlemen, the President of the United States of America."

A murmur rippled through the hall, and at that moment there were more people glued to their television sets than at any other time in the history of the world.

Two thousand puzzled eyes strained.   Kershaw attempted to mutter something that got stuck in his throat. Secretary Blankenship anxiously glanced at the Speaker knowing something was amiss.   Countless Americans watching at home sat glued to their couches wondering what was taking place.

From behind the door keeper, a disheveled man walked into the chamber. He was diminished by the oversized coat and the mismatched trousers gathered at the waist with a piece of rope. The shirt, once white, frayed at the collar, was cinched with a necktie tied with a double Windsor. The face was shadowed by a wide brimmed felt hat. His appearance spelled vagrant, but the confidence in his stride conveyed an attitude more compelling. Everyone, viewers included, sensed the contradiction and felt a cold chill as the situation convulsed out of balance. Nobody in the chamber moved.

"Mr. Door Keeper, I demand to know the reason for this interruption," Kershaw shouted indignantly. The imposter, complete with Secret Service escort, continued his walk down the center aisle. After he had progressed halfway, he began to unwrap himself. First the oversized jacket, revealing the frayed and not so white shirt. The checkered trousers, clean but worn, and the makeshift belt were in full view. Next he removed his hat which had been pulled down over his ears. Standing between the two Secret Service men was a man who appeared to be an unshaved version of President Thomas Glenelly. With that, the walls of the chambers seemingly contracted three inches, sucked inward by the group gasp from everybody in the room. It was President Glenelly, alive and well.

As Glenelly once again became recognizable a round of applause began to swell throughout the chamber. Starting in the far corner as a few members applauded, the ovation quickly swept through the chamber. Visitors in the gallery unable to see what was happening below, leaned over the rail for a better view.

Three Secret Service agents entered the chamber from the cloak room. They positioned themselves to the side of the speaking podium, and around Judson Kershaw. This conspirator was not going to escape on national television.

Kershaw and Blankenship exchanged frightened glances as Glenelly neared the platform. Not knowing what else to do, Kershaw gathered his address and slowly stepped off the podium. The Secret Service agents were waiting and firmly gripped him around the upper arm and led him toward the cloak room.

Glenelly waited for Judson Kershaw to be removed from the room before he took center stage. Finally, walking up to the podium, he pulled a folded piece of paper from his pocket and placed it on the lectern. Looking out over the crowd, he saw many faces. Some allies, some political opponents, but all seemed genuinely happy to see him. The gathering in the room and the viewers at home did not know what had occurred during the last week, but each waited with mixed excitement and patience for an explanation that would make sense of what they had just witnessed.

"Ladies and gentlemen," Glenelly began roughly and coughed. "First of all, please forgive this cold. Second of all, despite the sound of my voice, I am happy to announce the rumors of my death have been greatly, and spectacularly, exaggerated." With that bit of comic relief, the room erupted into laughter and another ovation.

Glenelly acknowledged the applause and tipped his head to his political cohorts and again called for silence. "Prior to this week, I have never knowingly deceived the American public or my family; however, after my timely and fortunate rescue a few days ago, I was convinced, that for the greater good, in order not to compromise the undercover investigation which reached the highest levels of this government, I should, for all intents and purposes, remain dead."

Near to tears, President Glenelly continued. "To the American public, but most especially to my family, my loving wife and two daughters, I offer my deepest heartfelt apology.

"During the next few days details of the conspiracy to assassinate the President of the United States will be made

public.   The Secret Service, unwittingly the scapegoat
throughout this ordeal, has in the last twenty-four hours acted
professionally and with complete loyalty.   In the morning,
press conferences will be scheduled. Prepared press releases
will be delivered to the networks, the newscasters in the
booths, and all major American newspapers providing them
with the complete details of the investigation.

"I do not wish to use this forum to attempt to explain
the events of the last few days. I will let the law enforcement
agencies involved do that. Rather, I wish to take advantage
of this gathering to announce a new social initiative.

"To all Americans, both in this country and abroad,
during the past few days, I witnessed, first hand, one of the
most devastating, the most threatening problem which tears
at the very fabric of the American dream: homelessness. In
this country, homelessness has reached epidemic proportions.
Some very good but unfortunate individuals have fallen
victim to failed social and economic programs of past
administrations. I place the responsibility for this plight truly
on my shoulders and at the feet of the government, not to
make a political point, but rather to remind all of us in this
room that we are here to serve the people. In this, I must
confess, we have been sinfully remiss. We are here of the
people and for the people."

The entire chamber, having overcome the shock of
Glenelly's appearance, broke into applause.

"In the next thirty days I will present to Congress a
comprehensive plan to tackle the issues of substance abuse,
job creation, housing subsidies, and of course to select a new
Vice President.

"To end on a less formal note, please know, I am not
a stand in. I am the real thing. I can not believe I am here
delivering this speech after such a dramatic attempt on my
life.

"Excuse me, I'm very tired, and I want to go home to
my family." As the president left the dais, the entire chamber

came to its feet with some very undignified cheering, stomping of feet and whistling.

Through all the excitement no one but electronic eyes saw the secretary of state exit the chambers.

43

Secretary of State Blankenship, taking advantage of the melee caused by Glenelly's resurrection, left his aisle seat. He walked passed the sergeant at arms and hurriedly moved toward the building exit.

Through the corridors Blankenship thought, "They have already taken Kershaw into custody. It will be a matter of minutes before they break him and he implicates me. The only answer is to leave the country. Once Kershaw tells everybody of our involvement, no gateway, regardless of size will be passable."

Fighting through a throng of reporters clamoring for a sound byte, Blankenship made his way to his car. On the beltway, he drove toward Northern Virginia. Falling into traffic, he cruised at a casual sixty-five miles per hour with the flow of traffic.

Chessie saw him drive up. He had also been watching television. Walking out to the porch, Chessie greeted the running secretary of state.

"Get me a plane, a plane. You've got to fly me to Mexico, South America, anywhere. Just get me out of the country, and do it now." Chessie just stared. "For God sake, why are you just standing there? Don't you understand what has just happened? Glenelly is alive and they've arrested Kershaw. We're next. We're to be implicated. Don't you understand?" Blankenship was hysterical and tears were streaming down his face. "Why are you so calm? Why are you just looking at me? Get me a fucking plane!" Blankenship was screaming.

"What exactly do you mean, we're in trouble? What does Kershaw know?"

"He knows about me, certainly, but you're in this. I'm not going down alone. If they finger me, you're going down, too. I won't do it alone. Get a plane. Get a plane..."

Michael Chessie heard everything he needed to know. He looked to his left as Blankenship plummeted on about escaping. Chessie nodded to Frank who had come around the side of the house. Frank took aim and put a hole into Blankenship's head with a small caliber revolver.

Later that evening, Darian Blankenship was found in his car somewhere along Highway 51. There was a hole in his head and a gun in his hand. The coroner ruled suicide.

44

It was nearly ten thirty. Jay Dawson hadn't bought himself a drink in two hours. There was no need, no opportunity. Once the story, as well as his picture, had been published in every paper in America as one of the main characters in the real life drama, Jay was unable to do anything for himself. Strangers everywhere he went made offers, gave him help, bought his meals, or his drinks.

Bob Gregg strolled into the lounge awash with his new found celebrity status. Just as Jay, he had been unable to do for himself all day. Gregg had been in debriefings through the afternoon.

"How did you put it together? Where did you hide the President? How did you gain access to the White House grounds? How? Why? When?" Those were the questions of the day.

Gregg strolled alongside Dawson and pulled up a bar stool. "Some day, huh, Jay?" Gregg asked.

"Yeah, some day all right. Debriefings, news conferences, phone calls. It's enough to drive you batty. My parents called and said they are barricaded in their house with the phone off the hook. It is a little overpowering," Jay replied.

Clapping Jay on the shoulder, Gregg cocked his head towards the rear of the lounge. "Come on. I know the owner here. I called ahead and had a room ready where we can sit and eat in peace.

"Hope you don't mind, Jay, but I invited my wife. Haven't seen much of her this past week." Dawson picked up his beer and followed Gregg through the crowd to the private dining room.

Several weeks later, the two men met again in Virginia. This time it was business. They had just finished their expose on the recent government conspiracy against the President of the United States, and against the United States and the world order. One of the national networks was to carry it on prime time television.

Both men were very satisfied with the product, for they had completed a good piece of work. Bob Gregg had come down to Jay Dawson's station early in the day to tape some voice overs. With that task out of the way, they sat in the viewing room and saw the documentary start to finish.

One of the network's editors was on hand and sat through it with them. Jay was offered a job as an investigative journalist with them in DC. Not having to think twice, Jay accepted the offer. Jay's boss knew it was coming. He was sorry to have to lose Dawson, but glad that Jay was closing in on his personal goal.

After the smoke cleared from the involved individuals in the President's cabinet, Bob Gregg received an award for

Meritorious Service, and was offered a promotion and a posh office in the CIA's hallowed halls. Bob Gregg did not have to think twice, either. He quickly turned down the offer, having looked forward too long to his retirement.

After showing the documentary, Jay Dawson took Bob Gregg to his favorite bar: McDougal's.

"I'll have me a scotch," said Bob Gregg leaning back and rubbing his stomach. "Make that neat, and make it double."

"My usual, Mic," said Jay ordering a beer.
"You might say this is where it all started," said Jay.

"How's that?"

"This is where I met Dragon Lady, Amanda Shahey."

"Ah, yes, and where she met her ultimate downfall, the foil who upset the proverbial apple cart, namely one Mr. Jay Dawson, electronic gadgeteer extraordinaire. Tell me, Mr. Dawson," Bob Gregg held the pepper shaker as a mock microphone, "do gadgeteers where mouse ears?"

"Hardly ever. We prefer antennae."

McDougal brought the drinks and the two men toasted each other's health and future.

"You know, despite what she did and what she was, she
was the most spontaneous, fun and uninhibited female I have ever had the pleasure of keeping company. What do you think will happen to the tattooed woman?"

"No doubt she'll be tried for the deaths of the agent and the ranger. Then she'll have to pay for truck theft."

"Truck theft? How the heck do you figure?"

"Her bike broke down before she got to North Carolina. She was joining up with some bikers down there, so after she put her bike in the garage, she stole some wheels to get her to her final destination. The little miss dumped the truck and had the gang bring her back for her Harley. That must have been when she headed for the hills. Anyway, she was gone long enough to frame you for the agent's murder."

"Which, by the way, I am now free and clear of any suspected wrong doing, thank you very much, Mr. Gregg," said Jay hoisting the long neck beer into the air to toast his friend.

"It's good our minds work as quickly as they do, or who knows what world order we might be living under right now," said Bob toasting Jay Dawson in return.

"Enough of this mutual admiration bullshit. When does the hunt begin for the Blackhawk?" asked Jay with a twinkle in his eye.

"Shee-ucks, Son," drawled Bob Gregg propping his feet on the chair next to him. "Ah am gonna' be a RE-tired gen'leman. And thank *you* very much."